Rand Stared Into The Eyes He Once Thought Guileless.

"Tara, you won't get anything more than sex from me. No gifts. No rings. No promises. And definitely no children."

Her breath hitched and her eyes rounded when she realized he'd accepted her terms. She blinked and swallowed and then dampened her lips with the pink tip of her tongue.

Hunger for her taste instantly consumed him.

Damn the desire. Damn her for making him want her.

Five years ago she'd made him forget every hard lesson he'd learned. She'd tempted him to break his vow to remain single and unattached.

He wouldn't make the same mistake twice.

Dear Reader,

It's not often a location won't let me go. But that's exactly what happened when my husband and I took a research trip to Miami and a cruise to the Bahamas for a book I wrote last year.

Miami is dynamic, exciting and diversified. I wish I'd had more time to explore the city and surrounding areas. I need at least a week just to sample the regional foods. And don't get me started on the shopping…. I'll need to leave hubby at home when I go back for that. ☺

I can see why Miami is the setting for so many movies and TV shows. On one hand you have the beaches, and on the other there's the money and power of the big city. I can't wait to return. In the meantime, I've indulged myself with setting THE PAYBACK AFFAIRS books in this great city. Hope you enjoy!

Happy reading,

Emilie Rose

EMILIE ROSE

SHATTERED BY THE CEO

Published by Silhouette Books
America's Publisher of Contemporary Romance

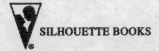

SILHOUETTE BOOKS

ISBN-13: 978-0-373-76871-4
ISBN-10:   0-373-76871-0

SHATTERED BY THE CEO

Printed in U.S.A.

EMILIE ROSE

lives in North Carolina with her college sweetheart husband and four sons. Writing is Emilie's third (and hopefully her last) career. She's managed a medical office and run a home day care, neither of which offers half as much satisfaction as plotting happy endings. Her hobbies include quilting, gardening and cooking (especially cheesecake). Her favorite TV shows include *ER, CSI* and Discovery Channel's medical programs. Emilie's a country music fan because she can find an entire book in almost any song.

Letters can be mailed to:
Emilie Rose
P.O. Box 20145
Raleigh, NC 27619
E-mail: EmilieRoseC@aol.com

To my parents, who have given so much love and support
even when it wasn't easy.
Mom and Dad, thanks for all you do.

Prologue

"**Y**ou will return to Kincaid Cruise Lines as acting CEO for one full year." The lawyer paused dramatically, his eyes finding Rand Kincaid's over the top of Everett Kincaid's will. "And you will convince Tara Anthony to come back with you as your personal assistant."

The words hit Rand like a bullet, knocking him back in his chair and punching the air from his lungs. "No. *Hell* no."

The lawyer didn't flinch. Years of dealing with Rand's bastard of a father had probably left the man immune to profanity and raised voices.

"Should you refuse, not only will you forfeit your share of your father's estate, but your brother and sister will lose theirs, as well. In fact, if any of you fail in your assigned tasks, then I'm instructed to sell all of Everett's holdings to Mardi Gras Cruising for one dollar. The business, the estate, the investment portfolio."

Son of a bitch. Rand slammed his palms on the table and shot out of his chair. He should have known the old man would find a way to pull his strings—even from the grave. "Mardi Gras is Kincaid's biggest rival, and the CEO is my father's sworn enemy."

"I am aware of that."

Clenching and releasing his fists by his sides, Rand paced the length of the Kincaid Manor dining room. He glanced at his younger brother and sister and saw more than grief and shock in their pale faces. He saw resignation, and in the case of his brother, frustration and suppressed anger.

They expected Rand to walk. The way he had five years ago. The fact that he'd failed to contact Mitch or Nadia or return their calls in the interim had no doubt contributed to their lack of faith in him, but he'd cut all ties because he hadn't wanted to put them in the middle of his war with their father.

Rand struggled to shake off the invisible straight jacket cinching tighter around him. He owed Mitch and Nadia, and not just for abandoning the family business.

He pivoted and refocused on the attorney. "Anyone but her. Not Tara Anthony."

Within three weeks of declaring she loved Rand and wanted to spend the rest of her life with him, the woman had gone after deeper pockets when Rand refused to cough up a wedding ring.

"I'm sorry, Rand. Everett insisted on Ms. Anthony."

His father would. The manipulative despot. He had always coveted whatever Rand had and then he'd taken it by fair means or foul and flaunted his successes like a cat leaves a carcass on the doorstep.

"And if she refuses?" Rand would make sure Tara did.

"Then you'll change her mind. Unless you choose to fail, there is no other option."

Another dead end. Frustration burned like acid in his belly. "I'll contest the will."

The lawyer didn't even blink. "Contesting by any of the three of you immediately results in forfeiture."

Rand struggled with the urge to punch something. His tyrannical father had closed the obvious loopholes before unexpectedly dropping from a heart attack in his latest mistress's bed three days ago. But there had to be a way out, and if there was, Rand would find it.

He planted his fists on the table and leaned toward the attorney. "Richards, you know my father must have been mentally incompetent to demand this."

"He wasn't crazy, Rand," his brother said before Richards could reply. "I'd have known. I worked with him every day. You would have known, too, *if* you'd stuck around." Mitch made no attempt to conceal his anger.

Nadia's head bobbed in agreement. "Dad was impossible, insensitive and immoral. But he wasn't insane."

A volley of curses ricocheted around inside Rand's skull. He straightened and nailed his brother with a hard stare. "Why aren't you protesting? CEO should be your job."

Mitch shrugged, but his jaw looked rapier-sharp. "Dad wanted you."

Rand couldn't contain his snort of disgust.

"That's a first. You were always his favorite and his right-hand man. I was his sparring partner—the one he liked to beat." Not physically, but in every other way. Sports. Business. *Women*. Until his father had taken their competition too far.

Rand looked from his brother to his sister. "This all-for-one garbage is absurd. He spent his life trying to drive us apart."

"And it looks like in death he's trying to bring us together," Nadia replied.

Richards cleared his throat. "Over this past year Everett

realized he'd made some mistakes. He wants the three of you to help him rectify them."

"So he won't eternally rot in hell," Rand muttered. A sense of doom descended on his shoulders. He was trapped. Like a rat in a maze. Exactly how his father liked it.

Whatever game you're playing, old man, I will win this time.

Even if it meant facing Tara again.

He squared his shoulders and looked his brother straight in the eye. "I'll do it. I'll come back to KCL, and I'll make Tara Anthony an offer she can't refuse."

One

The doorbell echoed through the two-story foyer, stopping Tara Anthony in the process of kicking off her shoes. An ivory sandal dangled from her toe.

Tightening her grip on the newel post, she debated ignoring her visitor and then groaned, stabbed her foot back into her shoe and rolled her tense shoulders. Whoever was out there had very likely watched her walk inside thirty seconds ago and knew she was here. As if to prove her point, the bell chimed twice more in quick succession.

No doubt she'd find another developer on the other side of the door, one who wanted to buy her lot, demolish her old house and build a minimansion in its place as had happened with so many of the neighborhood properties. This section of Miami had become an increasingly desirable location lately. But she couldn't sell. She'd promised her mother she'd hold on to the house. Just in case.

Tara pushed back her hair and sighed. She wanted this rotten day to end, and she wasn't up for a pushy sales pitch tonight. But apparently, her hot bath and the pint of Ben & Jerry's she'd planned to have for dinner would have to wait.

Not for long.

Tomorrow she'd buy a bigger No Soliciting sign.

Resolved to deal with her uninvited guest as quickly as possible, she crossed the foyer and yanked open the door. She reeled back in shock at the sight of the tall, broad-shouldered man filling the opening.

"Rand," his name poured from her in a lung-deflating whisper.

An evening breeze ruffled short, straight hair the color of dark chocolate, and his narrowed hazel eyes raked her from head to toe and back.

Emotions tumbled over her like raging river rapids. Shame. Pain. Anger. But something warm and welcoming spurted through her, too. *Love?* Could there be a lingering trace of that misplaced sentiment in her veins?

Surely you aren't still stuck on a man you haven't seen or spoken to in five years?

"May I come in?"

So polite, that deep, rich, goose-bump-raising voice. He hadn't been polite the last time she'd seen him. That day his tone had been cold, cutting and cruel.

You didn't waste any time, did you? You couldn't hook me so you went after deeper pockets. But the joke's on dear ol' dad. He wants you because he thinks I do. But I've already had you, Tara. And finished with you. He's welcome to my leftovers.

The chill that had seeped into her bones that night at Kincaid Manor returned. Wrapping her arms around her chest, she crammed the memories back into their dark closet and focused on the man in front of her.

"What do you want, Rand?"

He looked stiff and perturbed in his perfectly tailored dove-gray suit, white shirt and burgundy raw silk tie, as if he didn't want to be here any more than she wanted him on her front porch. "To discuss my father's final demands."

Everett Kincaid. One of the low points in Tara's life. "I heard he'd passed away. I'm sorry for your loss."

Rand didn't look mournful. "His will involves you."

Everett always had been kind to her, but why would her former boss leave her a bequest? Especially after the way they'd parted. "He left me something?"

Rand's lips flattened into a thin line and his square jaw shifted to an antagonistic angle. "No, but unless you agree to his terms we'll lose everything."

Talk about dramatic. She barely managed not to roll her eyes. And then, puzzled, she frowned. Rand had never been the over-the-top kind. He'd been very straightforward about what he wanted. And what he didn't.

She tucked a curl behind her ear and wondered if he noticed she'd cut her hair or that she'd lost weight since they'd been an item. Or had he slept with so many women that the features blurred together into a homogeneous female form? Had she even left a mark in his memory?

His lousy relationship track record hadn't kept her from falling in love with him five years ago, but back then she'd been young, shy and an impossibly naive twenty-four. She wasn't any of those things anymore. Watching her mother die slowly and painfully had aged Tara what felt like decades.

She should boot Rand and the memories associated with their brief affair right off her property, but curiosity got the better of her. She opened the door farther. "Come in."

His brisk stride carried him past her and straight into the

den. The same cologne he used to wear encircled her like a long-lost friend. A friend who'd stabbed her in the back.

No, that wasn't right. Rand had told her before their first date that he wasn't interested in forever. She was the one who'd broken the rules by getting emotionally involved. But how could she help herself when he'd been everything she'd ever dreamed of in a man? Fun, sexy, intelligent, attentive, gentle, good in bed. Correction. Amazing in bed.

She couldn't help wondering if she could have changed his mind about their future had she kept her mouth shut and let the love and trust sneak up on him. But she'd never know because three months into their affair she'd slipped up after making love and blathered out her feelings for him and her dreams for their future like the besotted twit she'd been.

Her ill-timed words had launched the next Ice Age and the fastest dumping in history. Rand had left her apartment so fast it's a wonder he hadn't burned tracks in her carpet. And then he'd left the country.

A frown line formed between his eyebrows as he examined the room's furnishings. "This looks nothing like your old place."

So he did remember. Her stupid heart skipped erratically. She scanned the room. The traditional furnishings were not the light-and-airy wicker and chintz she'd had in her apartment. "It's my mother's house and it was my grandparents' before it became hers."

His gaze sharpened and shot to the archway leading to the kitchen. "Is your mother at home?"

Tara's heart squeezed with pain and guilt that seemed like they would never end. "She's dead."

"Recently?"

She gave him points for trying to be civil, but she didn't want to discuss her mother with him. The wound was still too raw. "A year ago. But that's not why you're here. Could you get to the point, please? I have plans tonight."

Sad, solo plans, but that was the story of her life these days. Other than a few regrettable exceptions in those lonely months immediately after her mother's death when Tara had needed someone to hold her, someone to keep the loneliness at bay, men had been a nonissue for her since Rand had dumped her. She'd never found the passion or the connection she'd experienced with Rand with another man, nor had she found the solace she'd been seeking on those lonely, regrettable nights. The physical acts with near-strangers had left her feeling emptier and more alone than before, so she'd quit looking.

Tension crackled in the air between them. Rand didn't sit. Neither did she. "Everett's will requires me to return to KCL as CEO—"

"Return? You left Kincaid Cruise Lines? When? Why? The company is your life, your legacy."

"Yes. I left." His expression turned even more formidable. The lines bracketing his mouth carved paths through his five o'clock shadow. She used to love to feel that stubble beneath her fingertips and on her breasts. The memories made her pulse quicken and her skin flush.

"My father insists you come back as my PA for one year."

Rand's shocking revelation made her willing to overlook the fact that he hadn't answered all of her questions. "Me? Why? And why would I want to?"

"If you don't, then Mitch and Nadia will lose their home, their jobs and everything else."

Regret settled heavily in Tara's chest. For three years Nadia had been her friend, probably the closest one Tara had ever had. But a fissure had formed between them when Rand abruptly ended his and Tara's affair, and then Everett's proposition had finished what was left of the relationship. Tara had been so filled with shame and self-loathing she hadn't been able to face Nadia—or any of the Kincaids for that matter—again.

"I don't understand. Why would Everett insist on me returning to my old job? And why now?"

"Who knows what was going through his twisted mind? He has each of us jumping through hoops. He's harassing us from the grave." Bitterness and fury vibrated in Rand's voice.

What had happened to drive the men apart? Rand and his father had always been competitive, but she didn't remember Rand hating Everett. It sounded as if he did now.

"Can't you do something about the will?"

He shook his head. "I had a team of top-notch lawyers go over every word. The will's airtight. I'll pay you ten thousand a month, plus benefits."

Her mouth dropped open. "You're joking."

"No."

That was double what she'd made when she last worked at KCL and more than three times her current salary.

It had taken Tara four months after she'd left Kincaid to find a job. It hadn't been easy without a reference, but she hadn't dared ask for one after the way she'd left without giving notice, without even returning to empty her desk. Her replacement had done that and shipped Tara's belongings to her.

By the time Tara had finally found a position, she'd wiped out her savings, given up her apartment and moved in with her mother. The new job had paid less, but Tara had taken it because of the flexible hours and the opportunity for telecommuting gave her the time she'd needed to care for her mother during the grueling courses of chemotherapy.

Tara definitely planned to leave her current job. Her newly promoted boss was an arrogant, condescending jerk who had decided Tara's "flexible hours" meant she was at his beck and call 24/7. She just hadn't worked up the energy to start looking for a new position yet.

But working with Rand again… Too risky given that tiny flicker of joy she'd experienced earlier. The man had already broken her heart once. She'd have to be a fool to return for a second helping of that kind of agony. She shook her head. "I'm sorry. I'm not interested."

"Fifteen grand a month," he offered without hesitation.

Tara caught her breath at the obscene amount and her knees nearly buckled. Carol Anthony's job as a hairstylist hadn't provided health or life insurance, and Tara had inherited her mother's debts along with her home and possessions. With that kind of money she could pay off the exorbitant medical bills her mother had left behind and stop the increasingly threatening collection notices.

She was more than a little tempted. But why, oh, why did it have to be Rand Kincaid making this offer? "It's not about the money, Rand."

He punched his fists to his hips, shoving his suit coat away from the flat plane of his stomach—a stomach she'd once been free to touch and taste. "Look, we both know you don't give a damn about me. But do it for Nadia and Mitch. They don't deserve to have the rug ripped out from under them. Name your price, Tara."

Tara wavered. Common sense said refuse. But a minuscule, insistent part of her reminded her how good she and Rand had been together. When she'd been with him she'd felt special and important, as if happily-ever-after might actually be possible.

She'd never had time to come to terms with his abrupt ending of their relationship. Before she could sort out her chaotic emotions her mother's persistent cough had been diagnosed as stage-three lung cancer. From that moment through the next few years Tara's life had careened out of control on a roller coaster of hope and despair. Every waking thought had centered on her mother's survival. There had been too many difficult decisions to make and so many fears to face. There hadn't been time to think about her own wants and needs, her broken heart, disappointed dreams or the man who hadn't wanted her.

And then after battling four long, torturous years, her mother had died. Grief and guilt had consumed Tara. Since the funeral she'd been too numb to do anything but go through the motions of daily living. Work. Home. Paying bills.

She'd clung to the status quo like a sailor hung on to a capsized boat, afraid to let go, afraid another crisis would drag her under. Inertia wasn't something she enjoyed, but even one more change seemed like one more than she could handle. That was the only reason Tara could think of to explain why she'd stayed at a job she hated and why she couldn't face boxing up and donating her mother's things or even moving the bedroom furniture her mother had used out of the dining room. She couldn't even open the dining room door.

She chewed the inside of her bottom lip and studied the man in front of her. Was Rand's reappearance in her life a wake-up call? An opportunity to get her life back on track? Hugging herself she stared at the picture of her mother on the mantel.

Live your life without regrets, Tara. Promise me.... Her mother's final words echoed in her head.

Tara had learned two very important lessons as she watched her mother bravely fight and eventually succumb to the disease that had ravaged her body. One was that life shouldn't be filled with regrets for the things you hadn't done. The second was that some things are worth fighting for.

Tara had failed on both accounts.

She hadn't been courageous or unselfish enough to buy her mother more time and maybe even save her life—a fact that would haunt her for eternity.

Second, she'd let Rand walk away. She hadn't fought for him—for *them*. She'd allowed his fear of commitment and his unwillingness to listen to her reasons for turning to his father destroy any chance they might have had for a future together.

Rand watched her silently now with no trace of emotion on his hard-set face, but she was absolutely certain he had felt something for her back then even though he'd denied any emotions deeper than lust. If he hadn't cared, he wouldn't have treated her so well, and she didn't think she'd imagined the quickly masked flash of pain and shock in his eyes that last morning. If his feelings for her hadn't gone deeper than lust, he wouldn't have been hurt by what had appeared to be a betrayal on her part.

Unable to concentrate with his intense stare nailing her in place and compelling her to accept, she turned away. She'd never expected to see Rand Kincaid again, and she could have survived without him in her life. But here he stood in her home. It seemed as if fate were offering her a second chance to make this right—to make *them* right.

Did she dare try?

It would be a huge gamble. She might fail and get her heart shattered all over again, but at least she'd have the satisfaction of knowing she'd given it her best effort.

But how? How could she reach a commitment-phobic man who'd walked away once already? How could she prove to him that good relationships could and did happen?

She peeked at his reflection in the mirror that hung behind the sofa and caught his gaze raking her body. Heat flared in his eyes and kicked her pulse into a faster beat. And then he realized he was under scrutiny and masked his desire. He held her gaze dispassionately, but the raw hunger she'd glimpsed gave her the answer she needed.

She'd start with the one thing that had always been good between them—the sex—and build from there. And this time she wouldn't blurt out her feelings prematurely and scare him away.

Her skin flushed and her heart pounded at the possibility of sleeping with Rand again. She would, ironically, be offering him almost the same deal his father had offered her. Move in, be her partner in *every* way, and she would help him with his problem.

Would Rand have the courage to accept where Tara had failed?

Blinking to break the connection, she wiped her damp hands on her dress, exhaled slowly—shakily—and faced him. "I'll come back to Kincaid on two conditions."

"Name them."

"One, I want a glowing recommendation from you in writing. In advance." If this gamble didn't work out, she didn't want to be forced into another low-paying, dead-end job. She had bills to pay and an obligation to keep this house.

"If I give you the letter now, what's to keep you from walking before the year's up?"

"My word."

He hesitated, his square jaw shifting. "Done. What else?"

Chaos clamored inside her. She licked her dry lips and smoothed her damp hands on her hips again. "You. I want you, Rand. In my life. In my home. In my bed. Exclusively. For that year."

Rand recoiled as if she'd slapped him. "That offer is not on the table."

She fought to conceal her pain.

Did you expect him to be thrilled?

Maybe not thrilled, but something less than appalled would have been nice.

But without their intense physical chemistry on her side, the odds of succeeding in this quest were next to nil. She might as well give up now and save herself the false hopes and heartache. Mentally and physically, she backed away. "Then I can't help you."

His eyes narrowed suspiciously and the gold flecks in his irises glittered dangerously amidst the green. "What is this? Another attempt to get a ring out of me? I've told you before, I don't do commitment."

No, and he never would if she couldn't get past the boundaries he guarded so carefully. Last time he'd never spent an entire night in her bed or even met her mother. If she wanted her plan to succeed, she had to find a way to slip past his defenses and make him a part of her life. But she'd have to be careful. Rand would bolt if he thought she entertained even the faintest hope for wedding bells in their future.

She held his gaze and forced a lackadaisical smile even though her nerves stretched as tightly as piano wires.

"I'm not asking for forever. Just twelve months. You're not so irresistible that every woman wants to marry you, Rand. You and I both know this job is going to take long hours and involve a lot of overnight travel. I already have no social life—and therefore no sex life. Whatever else may have been lacking between us, the sex was always good."

Raw, urgent hunger exploded in his eyes and his chest expanded on a swiftly drawn breath. Her heart missed a beat.

He remembered their passion.

And that subtle reaction gave her hope and the grit to press on. She lifted her chin and squared her shoulders. "When do we start?"

What man in his right mind would refuse sex with a beautiful woman he desired?

He would.

"I can't give you what you want." Rand forced the words through a locked jaw.

Tara lifted a hand and tucked a golden curl behind her ear. Rand clenched his fingers on the memory of how soft her hair had been against his skin and tangled around his hands and wrists. While part of him mourned the long, loose curls, he had to admit the way the chin-length style bared her neck and shoulders was sexy as hell. Professional, but just tousled enough that a man knew she wouldn't mind him messing her up.

"Sex?" Her lips stretched in a tight smile.

"Love." He almost couldn't say the word. He didn't do love. Would never do love.

He was, according to his family, a carbon copy of his father. He'd learned the hard way not to allow himself the luxury of the destructive sentiment.

He'd seen how loving his unfaithful father had destroyed his mother and driven her to take her own life. And Rand had repeated the pattern when he'd broken up with his high school girlfriend before going away to college because he'd wanted to experience all the campus—meaning the female students— had to offer.

He was a selfish bastard, and because of that Serita had swallowed a bunch of pills that night after he'd left her. She'd been luckier than his mother. Someone had found her and called 911 before it was too late. Serita had survived loving a callous Kincaid.

"Ah. This is about what I said that night." Tara ducked her head, but not fast enough to conceal her pink cheeks. And then she lifted her chin and met his gaze. Her eyes were such an intense cobalt-blue that when they'd first met he'd believed them to be colored contacts. He'd been wrong. "I goofed, okay? If you'd hung around long enough for me to apologize and explain that I was lost in the moment—"

"Lost in the moment? You said you loved me, that you wanted to marry me and have my children. You practically named them."

The minute she'd said those words he'd bolted—to protect her from the curse of loving a Kincaid. And he'd worried about her for three solid weeks before returning to find her sneaking out of his father's suite after midnight.

Tara Anthony had played him for a fool and he'd fallen for her innocent act. Never again.

Her color darkened and her gaze bounced away again. "Um, yeah. Sorry about that. But you're…really good in bed."

Once more looking directly at him she added, "We can live here or at your condo. Either place is about the same distance from the office."

Every cell inside him balked. "I'm not playing house with you."

"Then I guess this discussion is over. I'll show you out."

Dammit.

Rand snagged her arm when she walked past him, and awareness shot through him on contact with her warm, satiny skin. The electricity between them had been there from the first time he'd shaken her hand on the day she'd signed in as his father's PA. He'd ignored the attraction between them—or tried to—for seven torturous months before saying to hell with it.

It had taken him a month to get Tara to go out with him and another one to get her into bed. Had she been playing him against his father the entire time?

"I no longer own the condo. I live in California."

Her eyebrows lifted and what appeared to be genuine surprise filled her eyes. "I didn't know you'd moved."

That reminded him of her earlier comment. He'd ignored

it before because he thought she was lying. "How could you not know I'd left the company? My departure from KCL had to have caused an upheaval, and my father must have hit the ceiling when I accepted a job with his West Coast competitor less than twenty-four hours after leaving KCL."

"I didn't know because I never returned to the office after…that night."

"The *morning* I caught you leaving my father's bedroom."

Thick lashes descended to shield her eyes. She stubbed a toe into the carpet. "Yes."

The same day he'd told his father to go screw himself because he was through screwing his oldest son. Those were the last words he'd spoken to Everett Kincaid.

"Why did you leave? My father wouldn't marry you, either?"

Her teeth clicked audibly. She jerked her arm free. "To borrow your words, that offer was never on the table. You need to leave, Rand."

He wanted nothing more than to walk out that door and never look back. Her demands were absurd. Was he going to meet them?

Searching for another option, he stared into the eyes he'd once thought guileless—man, he'd been an idiot—and came up empty. For Mitch's and Nadia's sakes he had no choice. Not one his conscience would let him live with. He wouldn't abandon his brother and sister again.

"You won't get anything more than sex from me. No gifts. No rings. No promises. And definitely no children."

Her breath hitched and her eyes rounded when she realized he'd accepted her terms. She blinked and swallowed and then dampened her lips with the pink tip of her tongue.

Hunger for her taste instantly consumed him.

Damn the desire. Damn *her* for making him want her.

Five years ago she'd made him forget every hard lesson

he'd learned. She'd tempted him to break his vow to remain single and unattached.

He wouldn't make the same mistake twice.

Tara Anthony couldn't be trusted, and he was and always would be his father's son. A chip off the old block. A selfish jerk to the core. A man incapable of fidelity.

One who could hurt a woman without a second thought.

A smile wobbled on her mouth. "If you're paying me fifteen thousand dollars a month, then I won't need anything else from you."

He ripped his gaze from her damp lips. "Two weeks. I have to fly home and wrap up loose ends. I'll be back on the sixteenth and our year will begin."

And he hoped like hell he didn't live to regret it.

Two

"Don't waste my time."

At the sound of his brother's voice Rand set his laptop case on his father's desk and turned toward the door. Mitch had followed him into the large office.

Rand had expected his brother to be glad he'd shown up not ready to pick a fight on Rand's first day on the job. "Excuse me?"

"Don't set up shop here if you're not going to stay the full year. If we're going to lose KCL, then let's make a quick, clean break and get on with our lives. Nadia is going to be miserable stuck in Dallas with nothing to do for twelve months. Don't put her through that if you're going to blow this."

Nadia's portion of the will required her to penthouse-sit and remain unemployed for a year. His sister would go crazy without something to keep her distracted from the memories that haunted her of the husband and child she'd lost.

Just one more reason to curse his old man, the sadistic snake.

"Mitch, I resigned from a job I enjoyed and put my condo on the market. I'm not going to quit. I'm here for the full three-hundred and sixty-five. If we lose KCL, it won't be because *I* failed to do *my* part."

Mitch's disbelief was plain on his face. "Why come back now?"

"Because this time he isn't going to win."

His brother didn't look convinced.

Rand shoved a hand into his pants pocket, withdrew his pocket-knife key chain and flicked it open. The blade flashed silver in the light as he pressed it to his fingertip. With the emotions churning through him he barely felt the prick.

"What in the hell are you doing?" Mitch demanded.

Red oozed from the cut. "You want me to sign in blood?"

"We're not kids anymore, Rand. Blood vows don't cut it. This is business. A multibillion-dollar business in case you've forgotten."

Clearly he wasn't going to erase five years of silence with their old childhood ritual. "I haven't forgotten."

Rand looked around for a tissue and saw nothing usable in his father's Spartan corner office. He dropped his knife with a clatter on the desk and put pressure on the tiny wound with his thumb.

Movement drew his attention to the doorway. Tara, in a pale yellow dress with her gleaming hair scraped back tightly against her skull, stood in the opening. The severe style wasn't unattractive, not with her bone structure, but he missed her golden curls. He shut down that port of thought. Her hair was no concern of his.

Tara's blue gaze traveled from his open knife to the small amount of blood on his fingers, then met his. "I'll find the first-aid kit."

Mitch's gaze tracked her retreat before returning to Rand. "Is she the reason you left?"

"I'm sure Dad spewed his own version of why I quit."

"He said nothing. That's why I'm asking you."

Rand tried to mask his surprise. His father had loved to gloat. "I left because he took our competition too far."

"How so?"

He stonewalled his brother with a look. Sleeping with KCL employees had always been frowned upon. Rand had known better, and to this day he didn't know why he hadn't been able to resist Tara's alluring trap. Since he hadn't been her supervisor, and therefore wouldn't technically be breaking any rules, he'd chosen to ignore company policy.

"What exactly do you want, Mitch? Guarantees? Fine. I guarantee you I'll see this through to the end."

"Why should I believe you? You walked away five years ago without a word. One day you were here. The next you were gone and completely incommunicado. Hell, I didn't even know if you were alive until your name surfaced on the letterhead of our competition." Mitch's eyes narrowed. "Rumor had it you'd run away with Tara."

Apparently the rumor mill hadn't known Tara was two-timing him with his father. "You should know better than to listen to rumors."

"C'mon, Rand. You and Tara disappeared on the same day."

Tara's gasp drew Rand's attention to the door. Her wide-eyed expression indicated she'd overheard. She searched his face as if seeking confirmation of Mitch's statement.

So she hadn't been lying. *About that.* She really hadn't known he'd left KCL.

"I—I have the first-aid kit. Let me see your cut," Tara said when he neither confirmed nor denied Mitch's statement. Her heels tapped out a brisk beat as she crossed the marble floor.

She set a small plastic box on the desk, opened it and extracted the necessary items, then held out her hand.

Rand cursed himself for being a fool. Why had he thought he could walk back in here and have things be the same—specifically his formerly close relationship with his brother? He regretted that casualty more than any other, but he'd sowed those bitter seeds with his silence, and now he'd have to harvest the crop of resentment.

He laid the back of his hand in Tara's palm and discovered that some things hadn't changed. Even knowing she was a liar didn't stop that same old zing from ripping through his veins. Her familiar sultry, spicy fragrance filled his lungs as she bent over her task. He welcomed the distracting sting of disinfectant as she gently cleaned the nick.

"Should I have the staff prepare your old suite of rooms at the house?" Mitch asked.

Rand's living arrangements were only going to add fuel to the rumors. Was that Tara's plan? Did she think she could use gossip to force him into a commitment? If so, she'd be disappointed.

Rand met Tara's gaze then his brother's. "I have a place lined up. Besides, you already have company."

Mitch's part of the will required him to play daddy to a child from one of their father's affairs, a one-year-old half brother Rand hadn't known existed until Richards handed out inheritance assignments. The boy and his guardian had moved into Kincaid Manor. Rand had yet to meet the kid. But in his opinion, the boy was better off not having Everett Kincaid in his life.

Tara quickly and efficiently bandaged Rand's finger, then released his hand and packed away her first-aid supplies without mentioning their cohabitation. If she planned to use it as leverage, then why hadn't she informed Mitch?

"Human resources has the first candidate for the director of shared services position downstairs. Which one of you is conducting the final interviews?" she asked.

"Show him or her to the conference room," Rand directed and looked at Mitch. "Meet me there in five. You know Nadia's current duties better than I do, and you'll be better able to gauge which applicant can handle them. But I'm sitting in. The COO should join us, too."

"There is no chief operating officer. Dad eliminated the position when you left."

Rand banked the information to deal with later. No doubt that action had launched its own series of rumors. "Then we'll handle the interviews together. As a team."

Mitch remained motionless for a full ten seconds, his gaze direct and hard. Rand held his brother's challenging stare and once again cursed his father for putting Rand in what should have been Mitch's job. As chief financial officer, his brother was the logical choice if the COO position had been eliminated—even if Rand had been raised to be CEO of KCL and had the experience of the top job with the competition. Mitch nodded and left Rand's office. Tara turned to follow him.

"Tara." She paused then looked at Rand. He lifted his hand to indicate the bandage. "Thanks."

"You're welcome." She bit her lip and shifted on her sandaled feet. "Did you leave because of me?"

The pain in her voice slipped between his ribs quicker than his pen knife had pricked his finger. He hardened himself to the wounded shadows in her eyes.

She was a damned good actress. Too bad her talent was wasted on him.

"You were merely the straw that broke this camel's back. You and my father deserved each other."

She flinched. "But I—"

"What, Tara?" he barked when she didn't continue.

Her chin and gaze fell. "Nothing."

"Good. Because the subject of the past is closed. Clear?"

Her shoulders snapped straight. "Yes, sir. Anything else?"

Rand scanned his father's—and now his—domain. He'd always hated this office. With its architectural glass-and-chrome desk, the bare, cold marble floors and the glass walls overlooking Biscayne Bay, the room looked more like a trophy case than a workspace. An empty trophy case. He eyed his father's metal mesh ergonomic chair with disgust. The old man's motto—"a real executive never looks like he's working"—rang in Rand's ears.

Not Rand's management style.

"Get me some furniture. Desk. File cabinets. Shelves. Tables. Wood, for godsakes. This pane of glass is useless. I want a decent chair—leather—rugs on the floor and comfortable visitor seating that doesn't look like acrylic urinals. And send the IT team up to connect my laptop to the company network. My father may have refused to work with a computer, but I won't work without one."

"Yes, sir." Her words snapped as sharp as a salute.

"I need hard copies of the press releases for the past five years, a current financial statement and a list of KCL's officers and division heads within the hour. That's all for now."

She pivoted sharply and headed for the doorway, but then stopped and faced him again without speaking.

"Spit it out, Tara."

"When are you moving in?"

Ah, yes, the other part of this ridiculous farce. Why had she demanded sex and cohabitation? What did she expect to gain if not a rich husband? He didn't buy her too-busy-to-date story. A woman who looked like Tara wouldn't lack dates or sexual partners if she wanted them.

But this time the scheming witch would fail.

"Tonight." Damned if the hunger for her didn't hit him hard in the gut. He desired her and he resented the hell out of her ability to yank his strings. "I want my own bedroom."

"But—"

"You'll get laid, Tara. But I won't sleep in your bed, hold you afterward or pretend we're a happy couple. I'm living under your roof because you've given me no choice. Don't forget that. Not for one second. I certainly won't."

She paled, nodded and quickly left him, driving home the fact that he really was a chip off the old block.

A real son of a bitch.

The voices in the KCL cafeteria petered out as soon as Tara entered. Heads turned and she found herself under the scrutiny of more than a hundred pairs of eyes.

She recognized a few familiar faces scattered among a sea of new ones and forced a smile. The buzz of conversation suddenly resumed. Apparently the employees who'd tapped into the gossip grapevine felt duty-bound to update those who hadn't.

Mitch's words replayed in her head. *You and Tara disappeared on the same day.*

She hadn't known. She'd deliberately sought a job outside the travel industry and had skipped the business and travel sections of the newspaper so she wouldn't hear talk about the Kincaids. She hadn't even read Everett's obituary. And now she and Rand were returning to KCL on the same day and working together. Tongues would wag for sure—especially if word of their living arrangements leaked out. That was one part of the plan she hadn't thought through.

Chilling doubt crept over her. Had she made a mistake?

No. When she'd been with Rand, he'd made her feel special, as though he couldn't get enough of her or wait to see her again. She'd felt the same way about him. He'd been a part of her life that had been carefree, happy and fun. Her life was none of those things now. She was tired of being alone and she wanted to feel connected again.

She only hoped those old feelings were still there, waiting to be nurtured back to life. From the quiver of awareness she experienced each time he was near, she had to believe that was the case. And today for the first time in ages she'd awoken looking forward to the day instead of counting the hours until it ended.

She crossed the bright and spacious cafeteria, and headed toward the food line. Kincaid's had always pampered its employees with first-rate amenities. Tara had loved working here.

Despite rumors from the business community to the contrary, she'd always believed Everett Kincaid to be a decent guy. Her former boss had offered her the gentle affection she'd never received from her own absentee father. When her mother was diagnosed it had seemed natural to seek Everett's advice. He'd offered a solution. Move in. Let him take care of everything. But the idea of sleeping with him when she still loved his son...

She pushed down the icky feeling and reminded herself Everett had been lonely and looking for companionship and a woman who didn't have her sights set on being the next Mrs. Everett Kincaid. Tara had been a logical choice. They worked well together and respected each other. And Tara had needed the kind of financial help only someone with Everett's deep pockets could afford.

But Tara ultimately hadn't had the stomach to accept his offer, and she hated herself for being weak when her mother needed her. Weak where Rand had been strong.

The hum of conversation died again as Tara picked up a tray and silverware. She glanced over her shoulder toward the entrance and saw Rand. Almost as one the other employees' gazes bounced from him to her and back again, like spectators of a tennis match waiting to see the next shot.

He spotted her and stalked in her direction. Tara's appetite fled, but she went through the motions of ordering shrimp scampi, grilled asparagus and rice pilaf even though her antennae were attuned to his approach. She calmly said hello to a few of the familiar line staff as if her heart weren't beating at twice its normal rate.

"My desk is gone," Rand said from close behind her—too close for a boss-employee relationship. She could feel his body heat and smell his crisp Lacoste cologne. Her mouth dried.

Conscious of their audience, she neutralized her expression, put a few inches between them then turned and met his gaze. "I had your office emptied while you were conducting interviews. Your new desk, along with everything else you requested, will be delivered at two. IT has your laptop."

"Good."

She gaped at him. Years of bottling up her emotions bubbled over. "*Good?* I worked miracles and all you can say is *good?*"

One dark eyebrow lifted at her vehemence. Okay, so maybe she'd been soft-spoken and eager to please when they'd dated before, and according to her mother, Tara had always had a tendency to avoid conflict and confrontation. But Tara wasn't the same starry-eyed girl Rand used to know—the one who'd been overawed at being pulled from the reservations center downstairs and moved to the executive suite on the top floor. Wrangling with her mother's multitude of doctors had given her a backbone.

"Thank you for being so efficient, Ms. Anthony," he said in a voice heavily laden with sarcasm.

She turned her back on him, but out of sight didn't mean out of mind in this case. Rand shadowed her through the line, his presence following her like a heat lamp.

When they reached the cashier he extended his arm past her, offering his company ID, which acted as both identification and debit card. "Put both meals on my account."

"You don't have to buy my lunch," Tara protested.

"I'm buying. Deal with it."

The cashier swiped his card without arguing.

Rand followed Tara to an empty table and sat beside her—close beside her. A prickle of uneasiness crept up her neck. "What are you doing?"

"This is what you wanted, isn't it? For everyone to see us together? Did it wound your pride when I dumped you, Tara?"

She searched his hard face for a remnant of the charmer she'd fallen for but found none. Back then she'd heard him described as gorgeous yet soulless, but she hadn't believed it for one minute. She'd seen his love for Nadia and Mitch and felt his passion for her in bed.

Had he changed that much? Probably not. The Rand she remembered hadn't been under as much stress as he was now. He'd recently lost his father, moved clear across the country and taken over KCL. Anyone would be cranky under those circumstances. She'd cut him a little slack.

"No one knew about our affair then, Rand, and no one has to know now."

"People knew. My father knew. And I'm sure human resources will spread the news that you and I both listed the same home address."

Another oversight. She hadn't thought about HR. "Your father had ways of finding out all kinds of information."

"He had spies."

"Oh, please. You didn't used to be so melodramatic. Everett

was a nice guy. People talked to him and he listened. Everyone except his competitors loved him."

"They loved him because he bought their affection," he said bitterly.

"That's not true. They loved him because he cared. KCL is a perfect example. Headquarters has trained chefs to prepare four-star-restaurant-quality foods at below cost prices, onsite child care, a medical center and a gym with personal trainers and dieticians on staff. And most of the company's employees could never afford to take a cruise on any of KCL's ships if it weren't for Everett's policy of deeply discounting employee rates."

She unrolled her cloth napkin and placed her silverware beside her plate even though the idea of eating repulsed her at the moment. Rand's proximity kept her nerves and her stomach tied in knots.

"Your father's ideology of a strong connection between work, family life and vacation time results in tight friendships with co-workers and a supportive community atmosphere. People like working here. They liked working for him."

With pity in his eyes, Rand shook his head. "He had you completely fooled. My father never did anything out of the goodness of his heart. There was always an ulterior motive and a price tag attached.

"FYI, Tara, it's cheaper to provide all the goods and services you mentioned, thereby keeping morale high and turnover and absenteeism low, than it is to repeatedly train new employees or waste money hiring temps who don't know the job."

What he said made a sick kind of sense. "You've become very cynical."

"Not cynical. Realistic. I was CEO of Wayfarer Cruise Lines for five years. I know what I'm talking about because I implemented the same programs myself and reaped the same rewards. Trust me, it's all about the bottom line." He picked up his knife and cut into his thick, juicy, medium-rare steak. "I knew my father. Better than you apparently."

If she believed Rand's account that Everett always had an eye toward benefiting himself, then she would have to seriously consider what Rand had said that morning when he'd caught her fleeing Everett's suite. Rand had claimed Everett was using her as a pawn in a game against his oldest son.

But she couldn't swallow that harsh tale because it would mean she'd completely misjudged the man she'd worked for, a man she'd admired and respected. A man she'd *almost* slept with. Never mind that Everett's proposition had totally shocked her. She was convinced he'd offered his protection and financial assistance because he genuinely cared for her and needed a full-time hostess. And he'd promised to pay for her mother to have the best oncologists available because he didn't want Tara to worry.

Right?

But a small part of her wanted to believe Rand, because it made Tara's inability to become Everett's mistress a smidgeon easier to swallow.

"This is your room."

Rand followed Tara into a decent-sized square room and set the two suitcases he'd brought in beside the queen-size bed. Not bad. More homey than a hotel, but nothing like his luxurious high-rise condo or the palatial Kincaid Manor. The double window was a plus.

Tara crossed the room and hung the garment bag she'd carried in from his Porsche in the closet. "This is the biggest bedroom. You can redecorate with more masculine colors if you want. With only Mom and me here, I'm afraid everything is pretty feminine."

He wouldn't be here long enough for the Monet decor to bother him. He hoped that once Tara realized she wasn't going to snag him she'd give up on her absurd scheme and let him get his own place. "Your father wasn't around?"

"He disappeared when I was seven."

Surprised, he looked at her. "You never told me that."

She stared at the beige carpet. "I, um, guess I didn't want to bore you. And you really never asked about my family."

An intentional oversight. Their relationship had been action-packed and tightly focused on their strong sexual attraction. He'd always been careful about revealing anything that Tara might inadvertently share with his father, and that meant avoiding personal topics. "Your parents were divorced?"

He wished his had been. And then maybe his father wouldn't have driven his mother to drink and suicide. Her death had been ruled an accident. But Rand knew better. He knew, and he should have found a way to prevent it.

"It's hard to divorce a man who's not here."

"He's dead?"

She shrugged and turned away to fluff a pillow. "I don't know. When I say he disappeared, I mean he literally disappeared. He left for work one morning and never came back. No one ever found his body or his car, and we never heard from him again. Mom and I moved into this house with my grandparents. It's where my mother lived when she met my father."

Sympathy slipped under his skin. He hardened himself to the unwanted emotion. Was Tara telling the truth or yanking his chain? He didn't know what to believe anymore. He'd believed her when she said she loved him. But then she'd turned to Everett days later, proving to Rand that his judgment concerning Tara was faulty.

He shook off the sting of betrayal.

"We stayed because Mom wanted him to be able to find us."

He stared in disbelief. "She thought he'd come back after twenty-odd years?"

She shrugged. "If he'd been injured or had amnesia or something, he might."

"Do you believe that?"

Her gaze broke away. She smoothed a hand over the bedspread. "I don't know. But Mom asked me to keep the house just in case, so I will."

He couldn't argue with illogical logic. "Bathroom?"

"Through there." She pointed to a door.

"Internet hookup?"

"Anywhere in the house. I installed a wireless network when I moved in. My mother was—wasn't well. I needed to be able to work wherever she needed me." The strong emotional undercurrents in her voice warned him to change the topic or get embroiled in an emotional tar pit he'd rather avoid.

Five years ago he'd been enthralled by Tara, now he felt entrapped. Last time he'd wined and dined her and swept her off her feet. This time he wasn't going to waste the effort. "Your room?"

"Across the hall."

"Show me."

She pivoted and crossed the caramel-colored carpet. Rand followed a few steps behind. His gaze dropped to her butt. She'd lost weight since they were together. He'd enjoyed her generous curves before, but this leaner version had its own appeal. Not that it mattered how attractively she baited her trap. He wasn't biting her hook.

A maple queen-size four-poster bed took up most of the space. His blood heated and need clenched like a fist in his groin. He didn't want to want her, dammit. But, to borrow a cliché, he'd made his bed and he'd have to lie in it. With Tara.

Consider it a job.

He'd had worse jobs than pleasuring an attractive woman. His father had made sure of that by making Rand work his way up from the bottom of the cruise line ranks. Not so for Mitch or Nadia. His siblings had never had to work in the bowels of a KCL ship or spend months sleeping in a window-less cabin.

Looking uneasy, Tara hugged herself and faced him.

Might as well get started.

He grasped her upper arms, hauled her close and slammed his mouth over hers. The initial contact with her warm, silky lips hit him like a runaway barge, rocking him off balance. And then the familiar taste, scent and softness of her flooded him with heat, desire and memories. He ruthlessly suppressed all three and focused on the mechanics of the embrace.

He sliced his tongue through her lips, taking, pillaging, trying to force a response and get the task done as quickly as possible.

Tara stood woodenly in his arms for several seconds while his tongue twined with the slickness of hers, then she shud-dered and shoved against his chest. He let her go and she backed away, covering her lips with two fingers.

What exactly did she want from him? She'd said sex. For a year. He'd give her exactly what she demanded. Nothing more. Nothing less. If she didn't like it, that was her problem.

He reached for his tie, loosened it then started on his shirt buttons.

Her wide gaze fastened on his chest. "Wh-what are you doing?"

"I'm going to *do* you. Isn't that why I'm here?"

She bit her lip. "Maybe we should wait."

He paused in the act of yanking his shirttail free. "Until after dinner?"

"Until we've…become reacquainted."

Her nipples tented her dress in little peaks, her breaths

came quick and shallow, and the pulse in her neck fluttered wildly. Desire pinked her cheeks.

"You want me—whether or not you're willing to admit it." And as much as he hated it, he wanted her. Physically.

It's a trap. Keep the hell away from her.

Not an option.

He closed the distance between them. "You made this deal, Tara, and I'm ready to deliver my end of it."

"I-if I wanted sex with a stranger, I'd drive to the beach and find one."

The idea of Tara with some other guy irked him. She was twenty-nine. Of course she'd had other lovers.

Including his father. He shoved down the disgust and dragged his fingertips down the smooth skin of her arm. He relished her shiver.

"But we're not strangers, are we?"

She jerked away. "I'll start dinner."

She tried to step around him. He blocked her path. "So you're calling the shots. I perform on command. Like a trained dog. Or a gigolo."

She gulped and briefly closed her eyes. "I had hoped the desire would be mutual. Like it was before."

"Before you slept with my father?"

She frowned. "I told you I didn't sleep with Everett."

"You forget, Tara, I know what you look like after you've been screwed. Your mussed hair, smudged makeup and the hickey you had on your neck that night, told the tale."

She sighed and shook her head. "Believe what you will."

The vulnerability in her expression nearly sucked him in. She lifted a trembling hand to brush back a loosened strand of hair. "We used to be good together, Rand. Don't you want that again?"

Did he want to be a gullible fool again? Hell no.

Given her betrayal and the Kincaid men's history with women, cutting her loose had been his only option. "I don't repeat my mistakes."

She flinched. "I never considered us a mistake."

He had to keep her happy or risk having her walk out before the end of the required year. He didn't know what game Tara was playing. She hadn't asked for romance when she'd brokered this bargain, but apparently she required a measure of pandering before they hit the sheets.

Fine. If she wanted seduction she'd get it. But that was all she'd get. She wouldn't get his heart this time.

Three

The hair on the back of Tara's neck rose. She didn't have to turn to know Rand stood behind her. Close behind her.

She'd been so engrossed in her reading she hadn't heard him return from Tuesday morning's round of interviews. He must have slipped in through the back door of his office.

He planted a big hand on either side of her blotter, trapping her against the desk between charcoal-colored suit-clad arms. Even with the back of her chair separating their bodies she could feel the heat radiating from him and smell his delicious scent.

She swallowed to ease the sudden dryness of her mouth. "Can I do something for you?"

"No."

"Then why are you breathing down my neck?"

"I'm reading over your shoulder." His breath stirred her hair and something inside her fluttered to life like a butterfly wiggling to get free of its cocoon.

"I'll send you the link to the company newspaper archives, and then you can read at your computer between interviews. Better yet, you can wait for my notes—the ones you asked me to make." She pushed her chair back, forcing him to move or have his wing-tipped toes run over.

"But reading over your shoulder is more fun." Rand stepped aside, leaned against the corner of her U-shaped workstation and smiled.

That familiar slow, seductive smile made her stomach flip. She studied the fit form beneath his tailored suit, his crisp white shirt and his neatly knotted black-and-gray striped silk tie. There was a difference in his body language today, one she couldn't decipher. It made her uneasy.

He was up to something. She could see the cool assessment in his eyes and behind that false smile. She'd sensed that same calculation in his kiss last night—a kiss that had been all technique and no emotion. If there had been even a trace of genuine passion in his embrace, she would have made love with him. She needed to be held that badly.

God, she was pitiful.

But the thought of having Rand "do her," as he'd said, repulsed her. She wanted him to make love with her because he desired her. Not because he had to perform.

If it weren't for the fire sometimes making the gold flecks glimmer among the green in his hazel eyes, she'd wonder if he found the prospect of making love with her as abhorrent as she had the idea of intimacy with his father.

If only she hadn't…

Live your life without regrets, Tara. Promise me.

She stiffened her spine. "If you need something to do, Rand, then go write my recommendation letter."

"It's written."

"I'd like a copy."

He eased upright and leisurely strolled into his office as if they didn't have a packed schedule for the day. She'd never known Rand to leisurely do anything…except explore her body. Heat prickled beneath her skin at the rush of memories and desire.

She narrowed her gaze on his broad shoulders and shifted in her chair to relieve the tension seeping through her.

Getting rid of him had been far too easy. His behavior confused her. Five years ago she'd loved Rand's focus and intensity. When he'd been at work he'd been all business, but when they were together and away from the office he'd been equally single-minded in his attention to her and his dedication to having fun.

Today he was muddying the waters, and she didn't know what to make of it.

She checked his appointment book. He had ten minutes before his next interview. With Nadia out of the office for twelve months fulfilling her part of Everett's will, Rand and Mitch had to hire her replacement soon. None of the pre-screened candidates human resources had sent up yesterday had seemed a good fit.

Tara turned back to her monitor and tried to concentrate on the words without much luck. Rand had asked her to list any pertinent happenings at KCL during their absence. She'd thought the company newsletters would be a good place to start. Instead, what she'd found—or rather what she *hadn't* found—disturbed her.

Rand returned, once more blocking her escape from her desk. "What's the problem?"

"Our departures from KCL are never mentioned in the first year's worth of company newsletters after we left. That's unusual. When someone leaves there's always a brief note stating years of service, company awards and such—unless the employee was fired. I don't like the idea of my co-workers believing I was fired. You shouldn't, either. It will make it difficult to gain their trust."

"My father was never one to offer excuses, explanations or apologies." Rand bent over her desk and scrawled his signature on a piece of KCL letterhead. He slid it across the glossy surface.

Tara took it, but didn't read past the header. "This is postdated."

"You think I'd hand you the ammunition to waltz out of here prematurely? If you quit early, we lose everything."

Which went back to their main problem. He didn't trust her. Had he ever? Tara sat back in her seat with a sigh. "I gave you my word I wouldn't leave, and I signed an employment contract. Don't you trust anyone, Rand? Anyone at all?"

"I know when to protect my own interests. Or in this case, Mitch's and Nadia's." He hitched a hip on her desk, invading her space with a long, lean knife-creased trouser-encased thigh. "Arrange a cocktail party for the executives of each of the brands by the end of the week. Plan to attend as my date."

"Is that wise? Us dating openly, I mean."

"I need a hostess, and you're the one who insisted on exclusivity."

So she had. And she'd occasionally provided the same service for Everett. Was that why her former boss had believed she'd be open to a more intimate relationship? "At Kincaid Manor?"

"Anywhere but there."

"Your father always—"

"I'm not my father. I don't need to flaunt my wealth or have a woman half my age on my arm to make me feel like a man. And I won't be taken in by a pretty face or a good lay. You'll do well to remember that."

She gasped at his rude comment. Was he trying to rattle her? If so, it was working. "Are you deliberately being obnoxious so I'll release you from your part of our agreement?"

He reached out and traced her jaw. Her pulse stumbled erratically beneath the slow drag of his fingertip.

"Why would I do that, Tara, when as you said, the sex between us was always good?"

Her mouth dried and her palms moistened. Arousal streamed through her. But suspicion dammed her response. She scooted her chair out of his reach. What was he trying to pull? First he'd flat-out refused to be her lover and then he'd accepted reluctantly. And now he was trying to seduce her?

His about-face didn't ring true, then she realized why. There wasn't any passion in his eyes despite his comment on their sex life. Rand was cold and distant—the way he'd been the day he'd climbed from her bed and broken her heart, and the day he'd caught her leaving his father's bedroom.

He wasn't at all someone she wanted to be intimate with. Not like this.

She didn't doubt he could make her ache for him even with this emotionless seduction. He'd always been a skilled lover. But perfect technique wasn't what she wanted. She wanted the unbridled passion they'd shared in the past, and it looked like she'd have to fight for it.

He glanced at his watch and stood. "We're going out to dinner tonight. Wear something sexy and low-cut if you want to get me in the mood."

He pivoted on his heel and stalked into his office.

Aghast, Tara stared after him. And then anger blasted through her. He'd just thrown down the gauntlet.

If she wanted to get him in the mood?

Oh, she'd get him in the mood all right. In fact, she wasn't going to be happy until she'd shattered Rand Kincaid's icy control and won back the man who'd given her the happiest days of her life.

Tara knew the minute her eyes met Rand's that her decision to fight dirty was the right one.

Tiny bubbles of excitement effervesced in her veins as she descended the stairs to where Rand waited by the front door. She could feel the heat from his unblinking appraisal warming her skin and her core. She forced her fingers from the newel post and indicated her dress with what she hoped looked more like a casual flip than a nervous flail. "Look familiar?"

"You expect me to remember your clothing?"

Oh, he remembered all right. His tight voice, flaring nostrils and the color slashed across his cheekbones gave it away. Those telltale signs made the hour she'd spent taking in the cocktail dress two sizes worth every second. Thank God for her grandmother's sewing lessons and her ancient sewing machine because Tara hadn't had the time, money or necessity to shop for evening wear since Rand had dumped her.

"I wore this dress the night we first made love," she told him anyway.

His lips flattened and his shoulders stiffened, but he remained silent.

"I fixed the tear. You know, from when you ripped the dress off of me in your foyer." His gaze dropped to her bodice as if seeking the mend, and hunger hardened his face. Her nipples tightened in response. Did he remember she hadn't worn a bra that night? Could he tell she wasn't now?

"Are you ready to go?" he asked tightly.

For the first time in years she felt alive and eager instead of numb. When he looked at her that way—as if he wanted to strip her and take her where she stood—she believed her plan to make him fall in love with her could actually work.

"Oh, I'm ready." She added a quick, mischievous smile to the words even though her stomach had twisted into a corkscrew of nerves. "Are you?"

She didn't mean for dinner. The desire burning in those hazel eyes told her the ashes of Rand's desire were far from cold.

And she had every intention of fanning the flames.

Even at the risk of getting burned.

He'd underestimated his opponent.

And that was exactly how he had to classify Tara from now on, Rand decided as he followed her out of the humid Miami air and into the cool, darkened house. She wanted something from him, and as with any business deal, he'd concede some points but not all. That way everyone left the bartering table satisfied.

Grace in victory wasn't a concept he'd learned from his father. Everett Kincaid had relished crushing and humiliating his adversaries. Rand preferred to allow his competitors to walk away beaten but not broken. Defeated, but not destroyed. In the tight-knit, almost incestuous cruise industry no one knew when they'd have to work for or with a previous foe again. Burning bridges wasn't smart business.

Time to seal this deal.

Moonlight shone through the living room windows, glinting off Tara's loose curls like moonbeams on rippling water split by a ship's bow. Before she could turn on the lamp he intercepted her hand and carried it to his chest. Her breath caught audibly.

She'd been leading him around by his libido for most of the evening, starting with a dress that brought back memories hot enough to cauterize his veins, followed by brushing up against him on the restaurant's dance floor until he was so hard he could barely walk back to their table.

She was good, *very* good, at luring a man into her trap.

It was time to regain control of the situation. He relaxed his clenched jaw and slowly reeled her in. His heart pounded out a hard-driving rock tempo beneath her palm. Snaking an arm around her waist, he brought her body flush against his. Hot, urgent desire pulsed through him.

Sex. Physical hunger. That's all this is.

And he could control that.

"Ran—"

He smothered her words with his mouth, stole them from her tongue with his. He didn't want to talk. Didn't want to be distracted from the job ahead.

She tasted of the tiramisu she'd had for dessert mixed with a hint of the sweet wine she'd sipped throughout dinner.

And Tara. She tasted like Tara.

Damn the memories he couldn't erase.

Her fingers fisted on his chest, but her resistance lasted only seconds before her body relaxed and curved into his, molding her soft breasts against a rib cage that felt so tight he could barely inhale.

He still wanted her even after she'd betrayed him, and the knowledge burned like sea water in a fresh gash.

Rand shut down his emotions and focused on his actions— actions guaranteed to seduce the woman in his arms. He swept a hand down her back, splayed his fingers over her butt and pressed her against his raging hard-on. Her quickly snatched breath dragged the air from his lungs.

Skimming his hands from Tara's hips to her waist to her shoulders and then finally her breasts, he mapped her new shape while he devoured her mouth. Hardened nipples teased his palms as he cupped and caressed her.

She broke the kiss to gasp for breath, and he dipped to sample the warm spot beneath her ear. Her skin was fragrant and satiny beneath his lips, tender and tempting against his tongue. Memories battered him. He bulldozed them back.

She shivered and drove her hands beneath his suit coat. Short nails raked parallel to his spine, inciting his own involuntary shudder.

Tara leaned away and stared up at him with her lips damp and swollen, and her breasts rising and falling rapidly beneath her low, rounded neckline. She pushed off his jacket.

He searched her face looking for signs of the conniving woman he knew her to be, but the shadows obscured his view. He grasped her waist and swung her into the moonlight. Dense lashes curtained her eyes.

She reached for the side zip of her dress, the one he hadn't been able to find five years ago. The sound ripped the silence, then she dipped her shoulders, first one and then the other. The black fabric floated to the floor with a swish, leaving her bare except for a tiny pair of black panties and her stiletto heels.

He gritted his teeth to hold back a groan. He even remembered her shoes. Or more accurately, he remembered doing her in those shoes. And nothing else. More than once.

Damn.

Heat and pressure built inside him until he felt like a Molotov cocktail—ready to blow with the slightest spark. He inhaled so deeply, so quickly, his lungs nearly exploded. Releasing the air in a slow, controlled hiss, he fisted his hands and fought the need to take her hard and fast where they stood.

Tara had been curvy and beautiful before, but now... Now she looked incredible. The curves were still there, only tighter, sexier. The moonlight caressed her breasts, the indentation of her waist, her hips, her legs. Oh, yeah, she'd definitely come well-armed for this mission.

He reached for his tie.

"Let me." She nudged his hands aside. Her fingers teased his neck with butterfly-light brushes as she loosened the knot, then she pulled the tie free like a slithering silk snake. She dropped it and started on his buttons. The roar of his pulse nearly deafened him.

Once she had his shirt opened, she closed the gap between them and strung a line of feather-light kisses along his collarbone. Rockets of fire shot to his groin. He ground his teeth together. She eased the cloth from his shoulders and licked the skin covering the pulse jackhammering in his neck. And then she nipped him and he nearly lost it. His fingers convulsed at her waist.

For godsakes, pull it together. It hasn't been that long since you've gotten laid.

Sweat beaded his brow and upper lip. He was hanging onto his control by his fingertips, and if he didn't take this upstairs, he was going to make an unforgivable mistake. Sex without protection.

He would never tie himself permanently to a woman. Or a child. He couldn't risk failing, either.

He tossed his shirt aside, swept her into his arms and headed for the stairs. But even within his grasp she didn't abandon her assault on his senses. She smelled good. Spicy. Sultry. Like sex.

Her arms looped around his neck, crushing her bare breasts to his chest, and the tip of her tongue traced his ear. Hot. Wet. She blew on the damp flesh. The effect was anything but cooling. A groan he couldn't contain barreled up from his lungs.

Tara had learned some new tricks since their breakup. Wondering who'd taught her made Rand's stomach churn like a concrete mixer.

In her room he stood her beside the bed. A small table lamp with a Tiffany shade cast a dappled puddle of Technicolor lights on the spread. One yank sent the covers flying to the foot of the mattress.

"Condoms." His voice sounded strangled.

She folded her hands demurely in front of her waist as if she were self-conscious. But he knew better. She'd demanded this charade. And that took balls. "In the drawer."

He pulled the knob she indicated with a glance, located the box and ripped it open. Extracting a ribbon of protection, he tore one packet free and tossed it onto the bed.

"Lose the panties. Keep the shoes."

A quiet laugh bubbled from her and a sexy smile tilted her lips. She looked up at him through her thick lashes and desire bolted through him, as jagged and searing as lightning.

He cursed silently. He'd said the same words to her in the past. Back when he was foolish enough to believe she was his every fantasy come to life. Back when he'd believed he could play with fire and not get burned.

Before she'd screwed—

Don't go there.

But the chilling thought brought him a measure of restraint. He wasn't going to think about…her other partners. Not here. Not now. It didn't matter whether she'd had one other lover or a dozen. He'd dumped her. Not his concern.

So why did the idea ride his back like a cheap wool shirt?

Get on with it. Give her what she wants until she begs for mercy.

She wiggled the lacy triangle over her hips and ankles then reclined on the bed with one knee bent. His gaze raked over her. Damp red lips, slightly parted. Taupe nipples tightly puckered on full, round breasts. The slight curve of her belly. An untamed tangle of golden curls. And legs…Tara had always had the most amazing legs. Long. Sleek. Toned. Her best weapon.

Her shoes—definitely do me shoes—were a reminder why he was here and what she'd demanded of him.

He reached for his belt with surprisingly unsteady hands. What was his problem? This wasn't his first trip to the sheets.

She watched his every move through slumberous eyes. His zipper rasped. He shoved his pants and boxers to the floor then had to sit down to remove the shoes and socks he'd forgotten.

She rattled him. He took a sobering gulp of air.

The mattress shifted beneath him. A whisper of warm, moist breath was his only warning before her lips brushed his nape. He snapped to rigid attention. Above and below the waist.

She cupped his shoulders then stroked downward as if she were reacquainting herself with the feel of his back, hips and buttocks. She hugged him from behind, aligning her hot naked curves against him. Her breasts burned his skin and her hands splayed over his lower abdomen. His muscles contracted, bunching with need beneath the soft scrape of her nails. Her thumb swept across his engorged tip, catching a slick droplet and rubbing it in.

A sharp stab of hunger had him sucking a swift breath. He bent to tackle his socks and shoes. Finally, he kicked both aside, then he turned and tumbled Tara back onto the pillows. He couldn't let her set the pace. Couldn't let her push his buttons. Couldn't let her make him lose control. Couldn't let her make him forget why he was here.

Do the job.

He kissed her on the lips. Hard. Fast. And then he worked his way lower. His tongue found and circled one nipple while his hand found the other. He plucked, sucked, rolled and licked until she squirmed beneath him and panted his name. Navigating south, he drew a damp line to her navel and then lower. Her fragrance went straight to his head. Both of them.

Every muscle in his body tensed. It took him a full ten seconds before he could think again. He found her swollen flesh. Smelled her. Tasted her. Laved her. Sucked her.

Too good. Too familiar. Too much.

He traced her slick entrance with his fingers and then plunged deep. Her hips arched. She dug her fingers into his hair and whispered his name. Using knowledge he thought he'd lost, knowledge he *should* have lost, dammit, he drove her relentlessly toward a climax with his mouth and hands.

Moments later orgasm broke over her, convulsing her body, contracting her internal muscles around his fingers. Her low, shuddery moan had him grasping himself with his free hand and damming the eruption about to happen.

He clenched his teeth until the white-hot haze ebbed.

What in the hell? He'd almost lost it. And he wasn't even inside her. He hadn't come prematurely since his teens. His *early* teens. And he'd almost—

He shook off the unsettling thought. Tara had always had that effect on him. She'd always made him want to rush. Going slow with her had been a challenge every time.

He grabbed the condom and shoved it on. And then he grasped Tara's buttocks, lifted her hips and drove deep into the wet, tight glove of her body. Buried to the hilt, he froze, locked his muscles and fought for control as sensation scorched a lava trail up his spine.

She's a job, dammit. Do her. Screw her. Forget her.

But she didn't feel like a job. She felt hot and slick and soft and so damned good. The fingers she dragged down his back sent sparks skipping down his vertebrae.

"Rand, don't stop. Please." She wiggled impatiently and clutched his waist. His brain short-circuited and his nerves crackled like downed power lines. He withdrew and surged in harder, faster.

Do her, screw her, forget her, he silently chanted with each thrust.

He tried to focus on the mechanics. His arms and legs trembled with the effort to hold back. His lungs burned. And then he made a mistake. He looked into her deep blue, passion-darkened eyes, and the hunger on her flushed face sucked him into a black hole of need. She cried out and her body quaked as another climax rippled through her.

Did she come like that with him?

The rogue thought slammed his libido like a submerged iceberg, stilling his movements, sinking his desire. Struggling to fill his deflated lungs and ban the repulsive image from his mind, Rand pulled away and sat on the edge of the bed with his elbows on his knees and his head clasped between his hands.

Damn. Damn. Damn. He couldn't do this.

When he had a measure of control he turned and looked at Tara, at her flushed face and her heavy-lidded eyes.

"Good for you?" He bit out the words.

"Yes," she said on an exhalation. Her brow furrowed. She rolled to her side and reached for him. "But—"

He shot to his feet before she could touch him and gathered his discarded clothing. "Then good night."

"But, Rand, you didn't—"

He slammed the bedroom door, cutting off her words.

No. He hadn't. But he'd come close.

Too damned close to forgetting why he was here.

Blackmail. His father's. Tara's.

And he'd almost forgotten who he was, what was at stake and that she'd lied to him before.

And that was a mistake he couldn't afford to make.

Four

Why had Rand left without finishing? Tara wondered as she swiped on her mascara Wednesday morning.

He'd been lost in the passion with her. She was sure of it. She'd felt his heat, his hardness, the rapid slamming of his heart and the trembling as he tried to slow his pace. And then he'd just…stopped.

Had she done something to repulse him?

Her idea of getting closer to Rand by getting *closer* to Rand had failed. Sex hadn't brought them together. It had driven them further apart, and now her emotions about last night were a tangled mess. He'd given her exactly what she asked for, but despite the climaxes, she wasn't satisfied. Physically or emotionally. In fact, she felt a bit…icky.

Not that the sex hadn't been good up until he'd walked out. But making love was supposed to be about *two* people. Not one. She needed more than just a superficial encounter.

She needed to know she mattered to someone.

In her experience Rand had never been the cuddle-until-morning type, but in the past he'd held her afterward at least until their pulses slowed and sometimes until she'd fallen asleep. But this time he'd—

She stopped midthought and stared at her reflection as realization dawned. She'd done it again. She'd let him walk away without demanding an explanation. Why?

Because she was afraid of what he might say.

The sobering reminder that she lacked courage when it counted chilled her. She'd learned the hard way that being a coward and taking the easy way out left too much room for regret. And hadn't she vowed not to do that again? If she wanted to make this relationship work, then she'd have to find the courage to ask what went wrong.

No more avoiding conflict. No matter how much she preferred not to make waves.

She put away her makeup and left her bedroom determined to ask difficult questions and possibly receive hard-to-hear criticisms. She paused in the hallway to gather her nerve and silence settled over her like a heavy, smothering quilt. An old, familiar emptiness filled the house. Rand wasn't here. She knew it even before she tapped on his door and didn't get a response.

Nonetheless she turned the knob and pushed open the panel. He'd made his bed. No discarded clothing littered the floor and no personal belongings cluttered the furniture surfaces. Only a lingering trace of his cologne hinted at his occupancy.

Desire and disappointment, relief and regret mingled in her belly. Since Rand had apparently left the house before she'd awoken for the second morning in a row, she'd have to ask her questions at the office. Not the ideal place for awkward morning-after encounters or private conversations.

Had he planned it that way? Was leaving before sunrise his way of keeping the walls between them intact?

She left his room and went downstairs. Last night's black silk dress draped the back of the rocking chair instead of lying puddled on the floor where she'd dropped it. Only Rand could have put it there.

She entered the kitchen. Like yesterday, Rand hadn't left any signs of his passing through. There weren't any breakfast dishes cluttering the sink or drain board, and the coffeepot stood cool and empty. If not for the slight tenderness between her legs, she'd believe she'd dreamed up his reappearance in her life.

She forced herself to eat a yogurt and drink a glass of juice even though hunger was the last thing on her mind. Her stomach churned over the encounter to come. She had to confront Rand and find out why he'd held back and why he'd left her. And then she'd find a way to make the next time better. For both of them.

Unfortunately, the pre-rush-hour drive to Kincaid Cruise Lines' towering waterfront building overlooking Biscayne Bay and the Port of Miami remained uneventful, giving Tara plenty of time to think about all the ways this affair could go wrong. By the time she pulled in to her assigned parking space her nerves had tied themselves into knots a Boy Scout would envy.

The security guard waved her through and then the glass elevator whisked her all too swiftly up the outside of the building to the top floor. Even the amazing view of the bay and the boats couldn't distract her from the encounter ahead.

She entered her office—the same one she'd used when she'd been Everett's PA. She was going backward, in many respects, to move forward. And yet nothing was the same. Especially not her.

The click of computer keys and rustle of paper carried

through Rand's open office door, affecting her pulse like a starting gun and sending it racing. She stashed her purse in a drawer, took a bracing breath and gathered her courage before crossing to the doorway.

"There are eight brands under the KCL umbrella," Rand said without looking up from his laptop. "All are profitable except the Rendezvous Line. Reserve the first available balcony cabin for us on a three- or four-day cruise. I want to see for myself why those bookings are down when that price point is the fastest growing market for our competitors."

From the look of his rolled-back shirt cuffs and the two to-go cups from a nearby coffee shop chain shoved toward the corner of his desk, he'd been here a while. "Us?"

His hazel eyes lifted and met hers coolly as if he hadn't been in her bed and inside her body last night. Unease prickled her scalp. Had sleeping with her meant nothing to him?

"It's primarily a couple's cruise. I don't want any fanfare or special treatment. I want to travel as an average Joe, not the company CEO."

The idea of taking a romantic cruise with Rand made her pulse flutter and warmth pool beneath her skin, but his all-business face erected barriers larger than the Rocky Mountains between them. She had to get past those barriers. If sex wouldn't do it, what would?

"I'll make the reservations in my name and through a travel agency if that will help with anonymity," she offered and he nodded.

"Give me the dates when you have them." His gaze returned to the computer screen, dismissing her.

Determined to get the awkward conversation over with before the rest of KCL's employees arrived or she chickened out, she tangled her fingers and approached his desk. "Rand, about last night—"

His jaw turned rigid and his head snapped up, corking her questions. His eyes met hers before slowly raking over her as if he were visually stripping away the red sleeveless dress and matching bolero jacket she'd worn to boost her confidence. His pupils expanded and her heart shuddered.

"What do you want, Tara? A roll on the company couch?"

Her breath caught and heat arrowed through her belly. A tumble of confusing emotions rumbled through her. She glanced at the leather sofa that had been delivered Monday along with the rest of the office furniture then back at Rand. Was he serious about sex in the office? Did she want him to be?

And how could she possibly desire him when he was being this cold and distant? Was she that needy?

He calmly checked his watch. "Mitch will be here in five minutes. You'll have to wait until tonight. Unless you want him to join us. I wouldn't want you to miss out on one of the Kincaid men."

His insolence left her speechless. Fury flooded her until she thought the dam on her temper would burst.

The slam of his office door made Rand wince.

He'd never deliberately humiliated an employee—or anyone for that matter. Humiliation had been his father's specialty. Rand knew firsthand. And he didn't like it.

But for a moment he'd seen an earnest and tender look in Tara's eyes that convinced him she wanted to make more out of last night than there was. He'd had to snuff that notion fast.

Last night... He shook his head. Last night he'd come too close for comfort to losing his head and forgetting what was at stake. Too close to forgetting she'd taken him in once before with her passion-glazed eyes and words of love.

Still, he'd been a bastard. Just like his old man.

Before he could rise to find her and apologize the door flew open and Tara stormed back through. She marched toward him with her fists clenched by her sides and angry red streaks marking her cheekbones.

Would she punch him? He deserved it.

She stopped in front of his desk, her body trembling. "I know what you're doing. You're trying to get out of your part of our deal with your rude, crass comment. But don't forget for one moment who loses if I quit. I just left one obnoxious boss. I will not tolerate another one. The only reason I'm not already cleaning out my desk is because I gave you my word and because Nadia and Mitch can't help it if their brother is sometimes a jerk. But if you make one more nasty remark like that, Rand Kincaid, I'll revoke my promise and I'll walk. And *you* will fail your brother and sister. Do you understand?"

Taken aback, he stared at the woman in front of him. The Tara he remembered had been soothing, soft-spoken and amenable. He'd never seen this assertive, untamed side of her before. The spark in her eyes and the strength in her spine looked more like the woman he knew her to be—one who could profess her undying love for one man then sleep with his father as soon as that man was out of town.

"I'm sorry, Tara. I was out of line."

Some of the starch seeped from her shoulders. She capped off her tirade by ducking her head and looking embarrassed. Her blush was so damned endearing and convincing, he almost wanted to circle the desk and hug her. And that wouldn't do. He couldn't fall for her trickery again.

"Completely out of line." She turned and left, brushing past Mitch on his way in with a brisk, "Good morning, Mitch."

"Hello, Tara." His brother stared after her then shut the door. "Lover's spat?"

"Explain that remark."

"You're shacking up with Tara."

The gossip grapevine thrived at KCL, and this time it had broken speed records. This was only his third day as CEO.

Rand clamped a hand across the sudden snarl of tension at the base of his skull. If he was going to keep KCL employees and the public from losing trust in the company after the change in leadership, he needed credibility. As Tara had already pointed out, a cloud of suspicion hung over their unexplained departures five years ago. Sleeping with his PA wasn't going to help matters. "Where did you hear it?"

"My PA picked it up in the cafeteria this morning." Mitch folded his arms. "So you did leave with Tara."

"No. I moved to California alone. But I am living in her home now."

"Rekindling the old romance?"

"There is no romance."

He considered telling Mitch about Tara's ultimatum, but confessing he'd become a pawn in Tara's game was as infuriating as it was frustrating. And arousing.

He hated that she'd backed him into a corner and turned him into her personal gigolo. Hated that, despite all he knew about her, she still had the power to make him want her. And he definitely hated the way his pulse had jackhammered and his blood had rushed below his belt the minute he'd heard her in the outer office this morning.

His sleep last night and his concentration this morning had been shot to hell because her breathy cries kept echoing through his head.

"Am I going to have to clean up after you the way I am after Dad?"

Mitch's reminder of their father's inability to be faithful to his wife or any other woman was exactly what Rand needed to hear to get his head back in gear. Even if Tara tried to sucker

him into a long-term relationship, Rand didn't have the staying power to make it last.

Like father, like son.

"How is it going with Dad's little brat and his guardian?
What was the tenacious aunt's name again?" Rand asked.

"It's going fine. Her name is Carly. But we're talking about
you." Mitch lowered himself into one of the sleek leather visitor
chairs stationed in front of Rand's wide mahogany desk.

Tara had indeed worked miracles on this formerly sterile
space. Besides the office paraphernalia he'd requested, she'd
added plants, art that actually looked like something recog-
nizable and a sofa long enough for him to stretch out on if he
had to pull an all-nighter in the office. An oversize ottoman
doubled as a coffee table and a foot stool. And the wooden
cabinet/shelf combo against the wall concealed a refrigerator.

Rand tossed his pen on his desk. "I can handle my own
affairs."

"Why did you leave, Rand? The truth this time. No BS.
And don't deny Tara's involvement. Your reaction to her name
at the reading of the will and the tension between you when
I walked in proves she was part of it."

Rand debated redirecting the discussion to the résumés on
his desk, but Mitch wore a familiar stubborn look on his face
that said he wasn't going to be diverted. His brother had a right
to his questions, and he needed assurances that Rand wouldn't
let him down this time.

And as much as Rand hated revealing the truth, Mitch
needed to keep a wary eye on Tara. If she was looking for a
rich husband, Mitch was just as likely a target. His jab about
Tara missing out on one of the Kincaid men had hit a little
too close to the mark. The idea gave Rand heartburn.

"When I returned from auditing the Mediterranean line five
years ago, I caught Tara leaving Dad's suite."

Mitch swore. "Not again."

"Yes, again." Tara hadn't been the first of Rand's lovers to end up in his father's bed, but she had been the only one Rand had given a damn about.

Had Everett pursued Tara or had Tara done the chasing? Either was a betrayal, but which was the most egregious? Tara's, Rand decided, because he expected no less from his father.

Rand stood and crossed to the windows to stare out at the blue-green water thirty stories below. "I was sick of his games, sick of him coveting everything and everyone I possessed. I didn't want to put you or Nadia in the middle. So I left."

"I was always in the middle, Rand, like a referee in a prize fight. But Tara was fair territory. You'd dumped her. Hell, I even considered asking her out. You have to admit she's smart and easy on the eyes."

Every muscle in Rand's body clenched. He spun and faced his brother with his fists ready. The challenge on Mitch's face dared him to argue. Rand couldn't. The moment he'd ended his affair with Tara he'd lost whatever temporary claim he had on her. Having no ties to her had been his choice. And it had been the right decision—the only decision—given the Kincaid history with women.

So why had seeing her with his father sucker punched him? And why did the idea of Tara with Mitch make him want to hit something?

Because she'd claimed she loved you.

And for a split second that night in her bed five years ago when she'd been spinning her fairy tale, Rand had believed her, and he'd wanted the life she'd described. Until he'd remembered who he was. *What* he was. A bastard who let people down. Just like his old man. He'd remembered what loving Everett Kincaid had done to his mother, and what loving Rand had done to Serita. He'd known he couldn't risk that with Tara.

And then he had recalled how his mother had told him she loved him minutes before peeling out in his father's prized '69 Jaguar XKE and plowing it into a tree at a hundred miles per hour. He'd remembered that Serita had called him on the phone and said the same words either right before or right after swallowing a bottle of pills. Had she intended those to be her final words?

But the joke had been on him. While he'd been agonizing over whether or not to risk loving Tara and letting her love him, Tara had moved on.

"Chasing Tara would have been a waste of time anyway," Mitch said, interrupting Rand's thoughts. "She still had it bad for you."

"Not so bad if she turned to Dad three weeks after we broke up."

"Whatever. Being second string to my big brother was a position I was tired of playing. I wasn't going after your girl." Mitch's bitterness came through loud and clear.

"She wasn't mine and you were never second string. You were the golden child who could do no wrong."

For a moment Mitch stared silently then he shook his head. "Why do you think Dad pushed you so hard, Rand? It was because he knew I idolized my big brother, and I'd have to raise my game to keep up with the standards you set. And you always aimed for perfection."

An invisible band tightened around Rand's chest. Mitch had idolized him and Rand had let him down by walking out and hauling himself to the other side of the country to nurse his wounded ego. "He yanked both our chains."

Mitch nodded. "Dad was a master manipulator. He had ways of getting what he wanted from each of us. He pushed and goaded you because you thrived on the competition. He was more devious with me because I never let him know when he'd pushed my buttons."

Rand cursed. How had he missed that?

Because you were too busy butting heads with the ol' man and too busy blaming him for being such an ass your mother would rather be dead than married to him.

And too busy hating yourself for being just like him. Selfish. Self-absorbed. Unable to love a woman the way she deserved to be loved.

Mitch stood. "It's against company policy to fraternize with a direct subordinate. Tara was as out of bounds for Dad then as she is for you now. Don't set us up for a sexual harassment law suit."

His brother would crack a rib laughing if he knew the price for Tara's participation was stud service. Rand ignored the rebuke and asked, "Since when did our father play by the rules?"

Mitch's gaze shifted to the trio of potted trees Tara had positioned in the corner to keep the late afternoon sun's blinding rays from creating a glare on Rand's computer screen. "Yeah."

The tone of that single word sent a prickle of unease creeping up the back of Rand's neck. "Is there something you're not telling me, Mitch?"

"I have everything under control. You need to make sure this thing between you and Tara doesn't turn sour. If you piss her off and she leaves before the end of the year—"

"She won't." He'd do everything in his power to make sure she didn't. He hated someone else holding the cards, calling the shots and controlling the outcomes. That wasn't his style. He liked having the upper hand. But the ridiculous terms of the will had him handcuffed, and for the time being Tara held the key. "At the end of the year KCL will be yours and Nadia's."

"What about you?"

For the first time in his life, Rand realized he didn't have a long-term plan. He hadn't thought beyond fulfilling his duty and not letting his father screw Nadia and Mitch out of their inheritance. He hadn't thought beyond beating his father at his own game.

Would there be a place for him at KCL?

Did he want to spend the rest of his life walking in his father's shoes?

He didn't have the answers.

"We'll table that discussion for now. We have work to do. I want Nadia's replacement chosen by the end of business today." He tapped the résumés on his desk. "One of these applicants has every quality we're looking for—if she survives the interview."

Mitch looked ready to argue, but Rand preempted him by pressing the speaker button. "Tara, please send the first candidate through to the boardroom."

"Yes, sir." Her snippy reply told him his apology hadn't totally placated her. He shouldn't care. He'd done what he had to do to make sure she knew she wouldn't fool him this time.

Tara Anthony was a complication he didn't need. Come hell, high water or hurt feelings he would keep his objectivity. Emotional distance was the key to surviving this year of playing house with a woman determined to land herself a rich husband.

He had plenty of practice with meaningless, no-strings sex. It was the only kind he'd ever allowed himself to have. He never got sucked in to his lovers' lives. They came together, satisfied each other's physical needs, then went their separate ways when the chemistry burned out.

This affair wouldn't be any different. He wouldn't let it.

"Waiting up for me?"

Rand's hard voice startled Tara. She pressed a hand over

her jolted heart and spun around. He stood in the open door of the dining room—the door she'd kept firmly closed for a year. His narrowed eyes pinned her in place.

"You startled me." Belatedly she remembered her tears and quickly turned back to her boxes.

"Tara?"

Ignoring the question in his voice, she swiped her face then snatched up the packaging tape and concentrated on stretching a long, sticky strip across the box's flaps. "I thought you were working late. You said it would take you half the night to go through the information I compiled on each of KCL's brands' executives, and you wanted to be familiar with each employee's history before the cocktail party tomorrow night."

He'd told—no, *ordered*—her to eat dinner without him and not to wait up. After the way he'd hurt her feelings and angered her with his nasty remark this morning, she'd been happy to have time alone. She hadn't even been able to escape him at lunch because he'd insisted she join him, Mitch and Julie, the newly hired director of shared services, for lunch at a South Beach Thai restaurant.

Her plan to regain what she and Rand had once had was on shaky ground because she couldn't get past his anger and distrust. She'd lost hope this morning after their ugly confrontation, and she needed to regroup and rethink her plan.

Maybe…maybe this new bitter version of Rand wasn't a man she could love.

Her fingers tightened on the tape dispenser and the serrated edge dug into her flesh. Exhaling, she made a conscious effort to relax her grip before she drew blood.

She could hear the sound of Rand's footsteps cross the hardwood floor. He stopped just behind her right shoulder. His scent and warmth reached out to her, and she had to fight the urge to turn and lay her head against his chest. Tonight had been hard, like saying goodbye to her mother all over again. But she'd known it would be. That's why she'd avoided this task so long.

"Why are you packing? You can't leave. You signed a contract."

"I'm packing up my mother's things. It's something I should have done a long time ago."

She chanced a peek at him from under her lashes. His green and gold eyes searched her face, then scanned the room, taking in the portable toilet, wheelchair and walker and the bedroom suite from Tara's old apartment.

When her mother could no longer climb the stairs, Tara had done her best to make her comfortable in this makeshift bedroom. Her mom had gone downhill fast in her last six months. She'd barely left this room except to be wheeled to doctors' appointments. She'd spent most of her time in Tara's wicker rocking chair in front of the bay window overlooking the back garden.

"She was handicapped?"

"She was dying. Lung cancer. Too many years of smoking." His impenetrable mask softened a little. "I'm sorry."

"Me, too. But it's time to move on. She wouldn't want me to keep this stuff when it could benefit someone else. It would have been cheaper to rent the medical equipment instead of buying it, but renting seemed like…" Her throat closed, burned. She stopped, swallowed, inhaled and then tried again. "Renting seemed like admitting it would only be a matter of time before I had to turn it back in. I wasn't ready…to give up."

He studied her long and hard, then glanced at the door and rocked on the balls of his feet as if he wanted to leave. Instead he sank back on his heels, shoved his hands in his pockets and inhaled deeply. "You never mentioned her illness when we were together."

"She hadn't been diagnosed then. That came...after...us." One moment Tara had been wallowing in heartache and woe-is-me, and the next her world had turned upside down.

Rand had been working overseas when she'd received the news, and with the ugly way he'd ended things, calling him hadn't been an option.

Forget it. There is no us. We have no future. I won't marry you or father your children. It was sex, Tara. Nothing more.

She'd had no one to turn to except the doctors, whose faces and prognoses had been grim. Panic had set in. She'd been so afraid of losing her mother and of the misery, surgeries and chemo her mother had ahead of her. The day after Tara had found out, she'd broken down in her office at KCL. Everett had whisked her to Kincaid Manor, where she'd poured out her fears.

And then Tara had failed her mother by refusing the one lifeline they'd been offered. Shame scalded her cheeks and weighted her shoulders.

She pushed back the pain and checked her watch. After ten. "I didn't realize it was so late. Have you eaten? I could fix something."

"I ate. Did you?" He indicated the boxes stacked in the corner with a nod. "Looks like you've been at this for a while."

"I...no, I haven't eaten. I...couldn't."

"You have to eat, Tara."

Her stomach seconded his opinion by growling loudly. "I'll grab something later. I'm almost finished."

She lifted another empty box from the floor to the mattress.

Rand laid his warm palm over the back of her hand, stilling her movements. "Take a break."

Her pulse did a quickstep, but despite her body's involuntary reaction, the idea of being intimate with him after what he'd said earlier today about sharing her with Mitch repelled her. As she suspected he'd intended his comment to.

She swallowed the lump in her throat. "I, um…don't need you tonight. So you can…go to bed. Good night."

His gaze held hers for a long moment. "Despite six months working in a ship's galley, I'm not a whiz in the kitchen. But I won't poison you. I'll scramble some eggs and make toast."

Why was he being nice after being so hateful this morning? She couldn't understand him. She bent her head and flicked a fingernail on the box flap. "You don't have to cook for me."

"Tara." He waited until she looked at him. His jaw shifted as if he were grinding his teeth. "You won't be any good to me tomorrow if you don't fuel up tonight."

She snapped her shoulders back. So much for believing his compassion was altruistic. "I'll manage."

"Is that how you lost the weight? By starving yourself? Get your butt in the kitchen," he ordered, then yanked the box from her hand.

She held her ground. "Why are you doing this?"

"Because I don't want you to be a liability."

"You don't want me period." She grimaced and bit her lip. She hadn't meant to let that slip. So much for holding onto her pride.

He caught her chin with his fingers before she could duck again. "I don't want to want you. That's a whole different story. Now get in there and sit down. I'll help you pack after you eat. Two of us will knock it out faster than one."

Emotion squeezed her chest and stung her eyes at this unexpected glimpse of the man she'd fallen for five years ago. Rand had always claimed to be hard-hearted and self-serving, but she'd seen past the facade to the man he'd tried so hard to hide. He might be a ruthless businessman, but no matter how many times he denied it, Rand Kincaid cared about others.

She studied his face. His lips were so close, his eyes so intense. He'd been a gentle and unselfish lover who'd coaxed her past her shyness and taught her about pleasure, about her own body. A less generous man wouldn't have bothered. She wanted to cradle his stubble-shadowed jaw and hurl herself in his arms.

Tonight proved the man she remembered, the one she'd loved, was still in there. Somewhere. All she had to do was draw him out.

Her waning hopes rebounded. All wasn't lost. And to borrow another of Tara's famous last words, tomorrow was another day.

And this time she wasn't giving up without a fight.

Five

"Could you hold me? Just for a minute?"

Tara's quiet question turned the dining room colder than a ship's freezer. Rand's muscles froze and his brain screamed, *No. Hell no. Don't fall for her tricks.*

But over the past hour of packing her mother's belongings she'd confused the hell out of him. Had she really been fighting to hide her tears and quivering bottom lip from him, or had she been giving the performance of a lifetime, letting him see just enough bogus pain to suck him in? Because her quiet, solitary grief had been so convincing she'd almost choked *him* up.

If she was really hurting and not acting, then a simple hug wasn't too much to ask. From anyone other than him.

But he owed her. She'd busted her butt at the office, doing more work in three days than most assistants could accomplish in three weeks. She hadn't complained once about the staggering workload involved in getting him up-to-date on the company, the twelve-hour days or the lack of breaks. She'd simply had snacks and drinks sent up from the cafeteria.

He flexed his fingers, knowing what he needed to do, what he *ought* to do, and dreading it. He opened his arms. Tara fell against him. The soft thud of her body hit him like a freight train. He reluctantly encircled her with his arms. Reminding himself this could be an act to lure him into her trap, he tried hard to stay detached, tried to ignore her scent, her softness, her heat.

But indifference was nearly impossible when he could feel her breaths hitching, could feel the tension in her rigid body as she fought to maintain control. Or faked it.

Warmth seeped through his shirt. Tears. The dampness spread across his chest and her body trembled against his.

He didn't do crying women.

This was exactly the kind of emotionally charged situation he avoided with his lovers. Normally he'd have been long gone by now. Watching Tara hug a sweater or a book or some other trinket to her chest and then carefully sort each item into boxes had brought back memories he'd rather not revisit. Memories of the Kincaid staff packing away his mother's possessions after her death.

Rand had wanted to keep his mother's favorite scarf, the one that smelled like her. His father had ripped it from Rand's hands with a terse, "What are you, a pansy-boy? Go to your room."

All Rand had wanted was a tangible memory of his mother. Hell, he'd been fourteen and drowning in the guilt of not being able to keep her from driving. Rand had known his mother was drunk and angry with his father about another woman. He'd known because she'd always ranted to Rand when his father screwed around.

Confidant wasn't a good role for a kid, and Rand blamed his selfish, immoral ass of a father for putting him in that unenviable position. But Rand hadn't argued. He'd been terrified his father would find out his role in not preventing his mother's death and kick him out.

By the time Rand had been allowed out of his room every trace of his mother had been removed from the house. Not even Nadia had been allowed to keep any of their mother's things.

He stuffed down the memories and sat on the mattress of the mechanical hospital-style bed, pulling Tara between his thighs. Every effort had been made to turn this room into a comfortable bedroom, but not even Tara's old headboard bolted to the wall could make this anything less than it was. An invalid's room.

He recognized the furniture from his affair with Tara, and memories flooded him. Memories of hot sex and of the playful bondage games involving that headboard. Memories that made him granite hard.

He shifted, hoping Tara would pull it together and break up the snuggle party. "You okay?"

She nodded and sniffed. And moved closer. Close enough that her hair tickled his chin and her scent filled his lungs. Close enough that her breasts pressed his chest and her mound nudged his inner thigh. Her heat burned him. And turned him on.

He moved to ease the pressure against his growing erection by leaning back on the pillows propped against the headboard and stretching out his leg. But Tara crawled into the bed with him and settled beside him. Her hips and legs aligned with his, and she rested her cheek on his chest. She wiggled even closer, reminding him she'd always been the cuddly type.

She was the only lover he'd ever lingered with, but in limited doses. More was risky.

So was this.

He wanted up. And out. Of this room. Of this house. Of this state.

This wasn't part of their agreement. He couldn't trust her.

The hardening flesh beneath his fly reminded him he couldn't trust himself, either.

"It's like sa-saying goo-goodbye again," she whispered brokenly before he could turn his thoughts into action and peel her off. "It's just so...ha-hard." The raw pain in her voice sounded genuine.

But then he'd been taken in by Tara's lies before.

Rand awkwardly patted her back, but said nothing. He didn't want to encourage any tearful reminiscences.

Tara's little gasping breaths eventually slowed and the fist on his chest relaxed. The tension eased from her body on a long sigh and she sank like a dead weight on his left shoulder.

Had she fallen asleep?

Oh, hell. Why hadn't he run the minute she'd turned those big blue wounded eyes on him?

Why hadn't he gone to bed earlier when she'd told him to instead of insisting she eat?

His arm tingled with pins and needles and started going numb. He stared at the dining room ceiling, at the chandelier hanging on a shortened chain above the bed.

He should wake her or at the very least dump her on her pink sheets and leave her.

But he remained immobile. He'd give her a few more minutes. If she was exhausted, it was because he'd worked her flat out this week. Once she rested she'd have more control over her messy emotions and be less likely to have another meltdown.

If the meltdown was real.

She might be looking for a rich guy to make her future easier, but the contradictions between gold digger, hard worker and a woman who grieved for her mother nagged him like a puzzle with a missing piece.

Minutes ticked past. He didn't know how many because he couldn't see his watch and there were no clocks in the room. His lids grew heavy. He rested his chin on her crown and let the flowery scent of her shampoo fill his nostrils with every breath. She still used the same brand. It pissed him off that he recognized it.

Getting caught up in a woman's Hallmark moments screwed with his detachment.

But he owed Tara tonight. Just tonight. For going above and beyond the call of duty. For giving KCL a year of her life. If she continued at the pace she'd been working, she'd be a bargain—even at the outlandish salary he was paying her.

But he had to make damn sure he didn't make a fool of himself over her again.

"It's 5:00 a.m. Why are you up?" Rand growled from the kitchen entry Thursday morning.

Startled, Tara looked up from the newspaper. "Good morning. If you're determined to get an early start every day, then I might as well join you. We can carpool and conserve gas."

Judging by his scowl that was the last thing he wanted to hear from her. "You won't get overtime for going in early."

She shrugged. "I didn't ask for it. I made *huevos rancheros*. Is that still your favorite?"

Not that they'd ever had breakfast together. Rand had never hung around long enough. But he'd mentioned it once. Funny how she'd remembered, but back then she'd hung on his every word.

His jaw shifted. "I told you, no playing house."

Was he cranky because they'd spent half the night in her mother's bed? When a bad dream had jolted Tara awake shortly after three she'd been shocked to find herself in Rand's arms. He'd released her, risen without a word and gone upstairs as if he couldn't get away from her fast enough.

"It's just breakfast, Rand. Eat and drink your coffee and then we can go. I'll fill you in on the arrangements for tonight's cocktail and dinner party on the way to the office."

"I'll take breakfast to go. You can fill me in later—when you come in at nine."

"I haven't come in later than eight one single day this week and you know it." She couldn't help pointing out that fact. "But have it your way. The resealable containers are in the cabinet to the left of the dishwasher, and the disposable forks are in the bottom drawer."

After filling a travel mug with coffee and packing the *huevos rancheros,* he paused by the table and scowled down at her. "If you think this sharing-and-morning-coffee routine is what I want, you're mistaken. You're better off sticking to the sex. At least I enjoyed that."

The old Tara would have let that comment pass, but the new Tara was turning over a new leaf. She was stronger and bolder now. Strong and bold enough to fight for what she wanted, and last night only reinforced her belief that Rand Kincaid was the man she wanted.

"But you didn't enjoy it. Why is that?"

His chin snapped up. "Because I couldn't help wondering if you'd cried out my father's name when you came the way you did mine."

She flinched at the unexpected lash of pain. "How many times do I have to tell you? I didn't sleep with Everett."

"You also claim you lied when you said you loved me and wanted to have my children. Why should I believe you're not lying now?"

She opened her mouth and closed it again. He had a point. She hated that he believed she'd slept with his father, but nothing she said was going to change Rand's mind. He had to come to that realization himself. And when he did, he'd realize how selfish she'd been. Her refusal to become Everett's partner in exchange for top-notch oncologists' care could very well have cost her mother her life.

Would Rand hate her for being weak? Because she certainly hated herself.

She sighed. "I'm not lying."

"Truth seems to be a fluctuating commodity with you. I'll see you at the office. Thanks for the breakfast and coffee. But tomorrow, don't bother."

"Any idea which heads will roll?"

Tara turned toward the familiar, raspy female voice. "Hello, Patricia."

Patricia Pottsmith had been head of human resources when Tara had originally joined KCL seven years ago. She'd been a cutthroat and ambitious manager back then, and her current position as vice president of the Rendezvous line implied that hadn't changed. She'd moved up the ladder quickly. Tara suspected it was because Patricia didn't mind who she stepped on.

"How about a little insider info for an old friend? A new broom always sweeps clean. Who is Rand going to fire?"

Tara didn't bother to point out they had never been friends. "Even if I knew Rand's plans I wouldn't reveal confidential information."

"I hired you and recommended you as Everett's PA." Patricia's haughty tone implied Tara owed her.

"I'm sorry. You'll have to get what you want from Rand. He'll be calling in each brand's management team for meetings starting Monday."

"Well, at least *your* job is secure. For as long as Rand's interest lasts, that is."

The bottom dropped out of Tara's stomach. "Excuse me?"

"Sleeping with the boss has its perks. I don't hold that against you, Tara. I've done it myself."

Tara tried to hide her distress and shock. Distress that she and Rand had become the hot topic. Shock that Patricia might have slept with Everett. Tara wondered again if she'd misjudged her boss. "Do the other executives believe I slept with Rand to get this job?"

Patricia rolled a narrow shoulder. "It's common knowledge that you never filled out a new application, interviewed or underwent a criminal background check and drug test. HR didn't hire you. You've been wasting away at a backwater small business since you left KCL, and yet you waltz back into one of the most sought after positions in the company— a company that prides itself on promoting from within."

To know this supposedly confidential information Patricia must have used and abused her HR connections. Tara scanned the group of sixteen men and women—the presidents and vice presidents of each line—who'd gathered in the glitzy private hotel dining room for cocktails and dinner. Their snide appraisals made her want to run.

The joy over an event well-planned and discovery of the perfect cocktail dress in a tiny boutique during a mad lunch-hour shopping dash drained away. Suddenly, her black jersey off-the-shoulder dress felt sleazy instead of subtly sexy. The garment exposed more cleavage than she was used to revealing. Not that the dress was daring by most people's—or Miami's—standards, but it was by Tara's.

She wanted a sweater. Or an overcoat.

And she wished Rand were here. But an international call about a problem at an Italian port had detained him as they were leaving her house. She'd driven herself and he planned to follow as soon as he could.

As if her thoughts had conjured him, Rand strode through the doorway. He wore a black dinner jacket over a white collarless shirt and black, sharply creased pants.

The years in California had been good for him. He'd always been confident, but he seemed even more so now. He dominated the room by simply being here, and it wasn't because of his position. It was the air of command he radiated. Conversations stalled and heads turned.

He scanned the room and his attention locked on her. He stopped in his tracks. His gaze slowly raked her from head to toe and back. At any other time his heated look would have made her shiver with awareness and pleasure. But not tonight. Not knowing that others thought she'd sold herself to get this job.

Yes, she was sleeping with Rand, but not because of work. It was because she thought they might be perfect life partners not convenient temporary bedmates.

"Excuse me, Patricia." Tara forced herself to move toward Rand. Her unsteady legs had nothing to do with the obscenely high heels she'd bought to go with the knee-length dress with a longer hem in the back that swished flirtatiously as she walked.

She stopped a circumspect yard away from him. "I've had the bartender serve drinks and appetizers. We're not far behind schedule. You'll still have time to mingle. All I need is a sign from you when you're ready for dinner to be served."

His eyes narrowed. "What's wrong?"

Had her tone given away her agitation? She made a conscious effort to blank her face. "They're waiting to see who you're going to fire. Let me get your drink."

He grabbed her elbow. "Tara."

She tugged but he didn't release her. His long, warm fingers held tight. She could feel the eyes of the executives on them. "Don't. Don't touch me. Not here. Please."

He frowned at her then shifted to stand between her and their guests, turning his back to the room and blocking her view of the executives and theirs of her. "I'll ask again. What's wrong?"

She hesitated, but if Rand was concerned with his credibility as CEO then he needed to know. "They know we're living together, and they think I slept with you to get this job."

His lips flattened into a thin line. "You knew sharing an address would cause problems."

"Yes... No. I didn't think it through. I didn't expect... animosity."

"You want me to move out?" His eyes searched hers.

If she wanted a chance with Rand, it was now or never. This opportunity wouldn't come again. She'd lived through watching her mother fade more with each passing day. She could handle a little gossip.

Live your life without regrets, Tara.

Lifting her chin, she squared her shoulders. "No."

"Then you have to suck it up and deal with their attitudes. You and I know the truth. We're both profiting from this situation." He waited until she nodded, then faced his employees. "Thank you for coming. I know you have questions. I'll answer as many of those as I can tonight. But first I want to thank Tara. She's put her life on hold this year for KCL.

"I recruited her and bribed her to return as part of the transition team because my father always claimed she was the best PA he'd ever had. In four short days, I've learned that if anything, he underestimated her worth. Tara has already become an invaluable asset to me. I place a great deal of trust in her opinions."

With a few words Rand implied the employees had better respect her, or else. After his gentleness last night, his support now was enough to make her eyes sting. She blinked to hold back the tears. She'd had to be strong for her mother for so long. Having someone stand up for her made her throat tighten.

No wonder she'd fallen in love with Rand five years ago.

"Most of you are familiar faces," Rand continued. "I look forward to getting to know the rest of you and learning how you believe you can increase sales in your brand. We have issues to address, and we will be making adjustments this year. But for the most part, KCL is on the right course. Your input is and will always be welcome. I have an open door policy, but if at any time you can't reach me, you can take your concerns to Tara and trust that she will relay *everything* you say to me. We work as a team."

Tara saw Patricia Pottsmith stiffen.

Rand turned to Tara. "I'll take that drink now."

She smiled at him and nodded. He'd called them a team. He couldn't possibly know how badly she wanted that to be true in every sense of the word or how hard she planned to work to make it happen. And every ounce of kindness he showed her only made her more determined to recapture the passion of their past.

Tara tapped on Rand's closed bedroom door.

Seconds passed, but he didn't answer. She knew he was here because she'd heard him come upstairs while she was removing her makeup.

Was he avoiding her? The evening had gone nicely for the most part. There had been some tension, but Rand had handled it well. And she wanted to tell him that.

She rapped again, harder this time. She was on the verge of returning to her room when the door flew open. A dripping Rand stood on the other side. Water streamed from his hair, cascading over his bare, broad shoulders and trickling through the dark curls on his chest and belly to be absorbed by the mauve towel encircling his hips. The dark hairs on his legs clung to his tanned flesh.

She jerked her gaze from his bare feet to his eyes. He looked annoyed, but that didn't stop hunger from swirling in her midsection. Not even the feminine, colored towel could lessen his masculine appeal. Bubbles clung to his neck behind his left ear. Shampoo suds?

She hugged her robe tighter around her waist, fisting her fingers in the fabric and fighting the urge to brush the bubbles away. "I—I'm sorry. I didn't realize you were in the shower."

"What do you want, Tara? A command performance?"

She flinched. "N-no. I wanted to thank you for tonight, for backing me. And I wanted to tell you that you handled the executives' anxiety better than Everett would have."

His jaw shifted and his eyes narrowed. "Thanks. Good night."

He pivoted and stalked back into the room without closing the door.

Don't let him walk away this time.

She followed him, admiring the wide, droplet-spattered V of his torso and watching as he grabbed another towel from the bathroom rail and briskly scrubbed the moisture from his hair and skin. The muscles of his back and arms flexed with his movements and her body responded by generating heat in her belly and her skin. "But you didn't have to lie, Rand."

He met her gaze in the mirror. "I don't lie."

"I meant about Everett saying I was the best PA he'd had."

"That was the truth. My father thought you could do no wrong."

"Really?" That meant a lot because she had tried very hard not to disappoint him after he'd taken a chance on pulling her from reservations.

She smiled and Rand turned to scowl at her. He scowled a lot these days. She didn't remember him doing so in the past…except for that last morning.

She cleared her throat. "Well…anyway, thanks for telling me and for your other compliments. And thank you for last night."

He shrugged one shoulder. "It was nothing."

"It wasn't *nothing* to me." She closed the distance between them and rose on tiptoe to brush a quick thank-you kiss on his cheek. But something went amiss the minute her palm encountered the steamy, damp flesh of his naked chest.

Rand sucked in a sharp breath. His hand gripped her waist, and he turned his head. Their lips met. Brushed. Clung. Separated.

Surprised by the sensual impact of what she'd intended as a friendly peck, Tara eased back and tried to catch her breath. His heart pounded heavily beneath her hand, racing almost as fast as hers. The gold flecks in his hazel eyes glittered and his pupils expanded with desire. An answering need swelled within her.

Moisture flooded her mouth. She gulped it down and gave in to temptation to reach up for the stray suds. She stroked them down his neck and across his collarbone, not stopping until her hands rested side by side on his chest.

She licked her lips. "I didn't come in here for this."

But that didn't mean she didn't want it. Want *him*.

Live your life without regrets.

Sliding her hands to his shoulders, she rose again and covered his mouth with hers. Rand didn't pull away, nor did he do anything to aid her. He stood as still as a statue. But so much warmer. Hotter.

Her pulse stuttered like the woodpecker that sometimes woke her by pecking on the gutter outside her bedroom. She sipped from Rand's mouth and then traced his lips with her tongue.

An almost inaudible sound rumbled deep in his throat. The fingers at her waist tightened. But he didn't push her away.

In their past relationship she'd never been bold enough to

take the initiative with him, but back then she'd been inexperienced and unsure.

She tasted him, sweeping the soft inner flesh of his lips and his slick teeth, and then she leaned in to him. His saunalike heat soaked through her thin gown and robe, scorching her breasts and abdomen and making her ache deep in her core.

Only Rand could melt her with nothing more than a kiss. Only Rand could banish the emptiness and loneliness clawing at her. She wanted him like she'd never wanted any other man. Showing him seemed…important somehow.

She lifted her head and sank back on her heels, then glided her hands over his chest, across the hard nubs of his tiny nipples and the sparse curls covering his pectorals. She traced the hairline leading to the towel with a feather-light caress. His skin goose-bumped and his stomach muscles contracted beneath her fingertips. His indrawn breath hissed.

She'd always loved touching him, pleasuring him, making this man who seemed so in control ninety-nine percent of the time lose it. He'd taught her how. In fact, he'd taught her everything she knew about making love, but she'd always been tentative and afraid of doing something wrong. In the end she had, but it had been her words, not her actions, that drove him away.

Leaning in, she painted a wet circle around one nipple and then the other. She grasped the towel on his hips for balance, sliding her fingers behind the damp barrier. The knot loosened. She tugged and the covering dropped to the floor, revealing his thick erection.

He wanted her. Wanted this. The undeniable proof stood between them.

Encircling his smooth shaft with one hand, she cupped him with the other and tested his length, his silkiness. His muscles turned rigid, the tendons of his face and neck strained.

She circled the satiny head with her thumb the way she knew he liked and relished his groan.

"Tara—"

"Shh. Let me." She sank to her knees and licked him from base to tip.

He jammed his fingers into her hair so swiftly she expected him to yank her away. But he didn't. Parting her lips, she took as much of him into her mouth as she could, stroking him, loving him. His texture. His taste. His response. Each growl and hiss and pulse rewarded her efforts.

She dragged one hand down a rock-hard thigh and skimmed it around to cup his clenched buttocks. Her tongue swirled around him and the fingers in her hair trembled. Each little quake teased her scalp and heated her core. She smiled and deepened her kiss, knowing he liked what she was doing.

Rand swore.

"Tara." He ground out her name in a command, a warning, a plea.

She dragged her short nails up and down the back of his thigh. The tremors spread to his legs. His toes curled into the rug.

She remembered his erogenous zones, the spots that made Rand shudder, and she shamelessly reacquainted herself with each one, lingering until his back bowed and his fingers fisted. He tried to pull away, but she cinched her arms around him and wouldn't let him go. And then he roared out his pleasure.

Moments later his hands fell heavily to her shoulders, then he cupped her face and urged her to stand. She rose slowly, kissing a path from his hipbone to his sternum, his collarbone, his jaw and finally his mouth.

Rand's arms banded around her, crushing her body to his as he kissed her so fiercely she grew dizzy and had to break away to gasp for breath. His hazel eyes burned into hers and his nostrils flared with each inhalation.

Happy that she could give him as much pleasure as he'd given her two nights ago, she smiled and traced a finger along his jaw. As long as they had this explosive chemistry between them, she had a chance to revive and improve on their past relationship.

"Thank you for being there for me." Her words came out choppy with emotion. It had been so long since she'd had someone to lean on. But she wasn't going to turn on the waterworks in front of him again. She'd done enough of that last night.

She wiggled free and made a beeline for the door.

"What was that about?" Rand's harsh voice stopped her before she could escape. Tara looked at him over her shoulder. Suspicion clouded his eyes, and it tore her heart. Why couldn't he trust her?

"I wanted to make you feel good."

The flush of passion had faded from his face and his lips made a thin, straight line. "What do you expect in return?"

She shook her head. "Nothing."

"Right." Disbelief stretched out the word. He closed the distance between them until he loomed over her. "You want me. I can see it in your eyes and the color of your cheeks. Your nipples are hard. I'll bet you're wet, Tara."

"Without a doubt."

He lifted his hand and grasped her shoulder. His thumb covered the racing pulse at the base of her neck. She shivered.

"I didn't say I wasn't aroused, Rand. I said I didn't expect anything from you tonight."

"But you wouldn't say no." The razor-sharp edge had returned to his voice. He dragged a finger to her breast, bumped over a tightened nipple, bisected her belly and grazed the sensitive area between her thighs.

Desire clenched her womb. But Rand seemed angry instead

of turned on and his anger wasn't what she craved. The gold flecks in his irises glittered, but not with hunger. This wasn't the same man she'd lost her heart to. This Rand was harder, less trusting and less charming.

What had made him that way?

"I wouldn't say no if I thought you wanted me right now. But you don't. And I don't want you back in my bed until you want to be there." Backing him into a corner and demanding sex had only thickened the walls between them. She had to give him space.

His eyes narrowed to slits. "What game are you playing?"

"No game." She stepped away although part of her ached to stay, to find sexual pleasure with him even though she knew she'd regret it later. "Good night, Rand. I'll see you in the morning."

She slipped through the door and into her room.

Gaining his trust would be difficult, but if she couldn't do that, then she'd never win his heart. Five years ago she hadn't been up to the task, but today she was older, wiser, stronger and more determined. She wasn't going to rush this time. She had a full year to accomplish her goal.

She wanted the man she'd fallen in love with back, and then she'd win him over.

Because this time nothing less than everything Rand Kincaid had to offer would be enough.

Six

The sudden roar of an engine broke Rand's concentration Saturday evening.

He looked over his laptop screen and out the window beyond the desk he'd set up in his bedroom, and spotted Tara with a red lawnmower on the back lawn. A floppy straw hat covered her hair and face, but her skimpy bathing-suit top and *short* shorts did a piss-poor job of covering her from her shoulders to the white sneakers on her feet. His gaze cruised past the curves of her breasts to her midriff and long legs and back up again. His pulse quickened.

He forced his attention back to the spreadsheet, but the numbers might as well have been encrypted. He shoved the pages away. So much for the financial report. His brain had been hijacked by his libido.

Again.

The entire week had been a challenge. Tara was everything

he'd said at the executives' dinner and more. Smart. Efficient. Productive. She seemed to anticipate his needs even before he recognized them.

She was also a distraction. Her scent lingered in his office long after she left, and he heard every movement she made on the other side of the wall dividing her workspace from his. He'd never had trouble blocking out his previous PAs' voices, but at this rate his open door policy was in danger of becoming the closed door variety.

She'd played him with the oldest trick in the book Thursday night. Seduction. And it pissed him off. Heat steamed from his pores and his body switched to red alert at the mental replay of her hot, wet mouth pulling a response from him. One he'd wanted to deny but couldn't.

Cursing his inability to block the images from his memory, he closed his laptop, and gave in to the temptation to look at her again.

What was it about Tara Anthony that made him ignore rules and good sense?

Tara swiped a hand across her forehead, driving Rand's gaze to the outside thermometer hanging by the back gate in the flower-flooded garden. Eighty-eight degrees. He drummed his fingers on the desk.

He'd been cloistered in his bedroom working for most of the day. And he wanted to stay here, avoiding Tara, avoiding the sexual craving her proximity caused, avoiding the memory of her talented, lying mouth. Avoiding the relationship he wanted no part of but she seemed insistent on forcing.

But his conscience wouldn't let him, and he couldn't concentrate with her making all that racket. He shot out of his chair, headed downstairs and plowed open the back door. He slammed into a humid wall of heat the second he hit the patio. Tracking the engine noise, he stepped off the hot flagstones and around a hedge of tall green shrubs loaded with pink blooms and buzzing bees, and jerked to a halt when he spotted Tara bent at the waist with one hand on the mower handle. The curve of her backside pointed in his direction, and her shorts rode up to expose paler crescents of flesh beneath the ragged hem.

His muscles seized and his eyes gorged. A burn unrelated to the evening sun baked his skin. He fisted his hands by his side against the urge to trace those untanned curves. Most women hated tan lines, but he loved them. That pale flesh signified something taboo, an area meant to be concealed.

Tara scooped up a yellow ball, straightened then tossed the toy over the six-foot wooden privacy fence separating her yard from her neighbor's. She resumed mowing, her long, lean leg muscles flexing with each stride.

"Tara." She either didn't hear him or ignored him. "Tara," he shouted.

She spun around so abruptly the noisy engine died. "What?"

The closer he got to her, the drier his mouth became. Her blue underwire top cupped and lifted her breasts like lingerie *or his hands* would, and her denim shorts were so old and faded it was a wonder they hadn't split at the seams when she'd bent over. On second thoughts, they hadn't torn because they were too large and barely clung to her hips. The waistband gaped to reveal her navel. Frayed bits of bleached fabric danced along the tops of her thighs in the slight evening breeze. A sheen of sweat glistened on her body, and a rivulet ran from between her breasts to disappear behind her loose waistband.

One tug and Tara's denim cutoffs would be tatters. Rand's fingers twitched. He swallowed, but the gesture did nothing to wet his dry mouth or douse the fire behind his fly. Neither did his gulps of suntan-oil-and-fresh-cut-grass-scented air.

"Why don't you have a lawn service?" The unwanted attraction pissed him off and his anger came through in his clipped words.

She shrugged, removed her hat and wiped her forehead with her forearm. "Too expensive."

"Not with the salary I'm paying you."

"That money is earmarked for something else."

"What?"

She shifted and the shorts slid south a fraction of an inch. Another wiggle of her hips and they'd hit the grass.

Was she wearing panties?

Was prancing around out here in her skimpy clothing part of her hook-a-husband plan?

As if she'd guessed his thoughts, she hitched up her pants. "Most of it's going toward my mother's medical bills. If I don't get them paid off soon the creditors are going to put a lien on the house."

"The house she wanted you to keep."

"Yes."

"Just in case your father came looking for her," he said, repeating her ridiculous story. "What kind of woman loves a man who walks out on her?"

"The kind who vowed to love, honor and cherish until death parted them. We never had proof that my father died. Mom kept her vow."

So had his mother, he realized. The sobering thought knocked Rand back a step. His mother had loved her jackass of a husband despite his repeated infidelities.

Tara sighed. "Rand, did you need something? Because I'd like to get this finished before the forecasted thunderstorms roll in."

As if to reinforce her point, thunder rumbled in the distance. Sweat glued the fabric of his polo shirt to his torso. "I'll hire a landscaping crew and have them onsite first thing Monday. You don't have to do this."

She shook her head. "Yes, I do. The yard is something my mother and I always worked on together. I need to do this. For her. For me."

Crap. Another Hallmark moment.

It was bad enough that pictures littered the flat surfaces in the house—pictures of the happy kind of childhood Rand and his siblings hadn't had. Pictures of the kind of life Tara had told him she wanted five years ago. With him.

Face it. She lied about loving you and you fell for it. Get over it and move on.

Curses ricocheted around his skull and every instinct told him to retreat inside and get back to work. She was sucking him into suburbia and into a relationship against his will.

He did not want to share her home, her chores or her life. But he could hardly sit inside in the air-conditioning while Tara toiled away in the summer heat. He wasn't a freeloader.

And since you're not paying your way with sex—

Dammit. He wasn't pissed off that she hadn't approached him since the night she'd blown his…mind. He didn't want to be her gigolo.

"How can I help?" The words clawed their way up his throat.

She tilted her head and considered him for several seconds. "If you'll mow, I'll handle the Weed Eater."

Rand studied the machine. He knew nothing about lawnmowers or mowing grass. Kincaid Manor had always employed a team of gardeners. Since moving out of the family house more than a decade ago, he'd lived in high-rise urban condos surrounded by concrete. If there had been any plants in his complexes, he hadn't noticed them.

But he'd spent one summer working in the engine room of a 160,000-ton cruise ship. He could handle one small push mower. "Okay."

Tara's gaze drifted over his shirt and khaki pants. She did

that often—looked him over from top to bottom. And his body reacted predictably. Every time. He resented the ease with which she pushed his buttons when no other woman's come-hither looks did a thing for him—unless he allowed it. Fighting the unwanted response, he shoved his hands in his pockets.

"You'll need to change first. You'll roast in long pants." Without waiting for his reply she walked away.

His gaze remained riveted to the sway of her behind until she disappeared into the shed that looked like a small chalet in the back corner of the property. Cursing silently, Rand returned to his bedroom, changed into an old sleeveless T-shirt, gym shorts and running shoes and went back outside.

Even before he finished reading the instructions printed on the machine's handle, he'd sweated through his shirt. He peeled off the soggy, clingy cotton and tossed it onto the patio, then bent and pulled the mower's cord. The motor sputtered but didn't start. He cursed and tried again. Another sputter. Another curse.

A slender leg entered his peripheral vision. He tracked that sleek, lightly tanned skin upward, past a shapely thigh, a hip, the indenture of her waist and the swell of her breast. Tara stood beside him carrying a Weed Eater and wearing safety goggles on her brim-shadowed face. She looked like a model from the pages of a handyman's sexy calendar—the kind a guy would hide in his gym locker or his garage. Any red-blooded male would want to roll in the grass with her in that getup.

"Have you ever used a lawnmower?" she asked, her eyes raking over his bare chest.

"No. But I can handle it," he said through clenched teeth.

She smiled and squeezed the two handles together. "Safety feature. If you let go and the handles separate, the mower shuts off. Now pull the cord."

He did, conscious of her nearly naked body beside him and

of those blue eyes tracking his every move. The engine roared to life. He fastened his fingers around the vibrating bar. Tara nodded and leaned forward until her breast bumped his elbow and her lips touched his ear. Fire sparked in Rand's groin. His hand slipped and silence once again descended on the yard as the engine died.

She dropped back on her heels. "Stick to the grass and stay out of the flower beds. I'll get the hard to reach stuff."

And then she sashayed away, leaving him to master the machine. She fired up the Weed Eater. The alluring play of muscles beneath her skin as she whirred her way along the fence enclosing the yard held him captive. She hadn't had those muscles five years ago. He knew, because there wasn't an inch of her he hadn't explored. With his hands. His lips. His tongue.

Rand blinked and pivoted away from her distracting presence. He restarted the mower and shoved it forward, focusing on plowing straight lines through the thick emerald carpet of grass. If he didn't pay attention, he'd probably cut off his foot.

The contradictions in Tara's behavior nagged him as he worked. She still drove the same car she'd owned when they dated. She wore old clothing better suited to a rag bag, did her own yard work and paid her mother's bills.

He glanced once more at the woman who'd blackmailed him into being her house and bedmate. Had he been wrong about Tara in the past?

No, dammit. He'd seen her coming out of his father's bedroom with a hickey on her neck, a flushed face and messed-up clothing. Regardless of what lie she'd concocted, she'd been intimate with his father.

Add in that she hadn't accepted the KCL job until Rand offered a salary that was quadruple the industry standard and agreed to play house, and it was clear Tara Anthony was up to something. The question was what?

She had to be looking for a sugar daddy.

But she wouldn't find one in him.

For Mitch's and Nadia's sakes Rand would be smarter this time around. Because he had a hell of a lot more to lose.

"Good morning, Rand."

Tara caught the almost imperceptible hitch in Rand's step and the brief flash of surprise in his eyes when he turned the corner into their office suite and realized she'd beaten him to work Monday morning.

Mouth tight, he nodded and resumed his course. He had to pass her desk to get to his office. "You're in early."

He'd hibernated in his room for most of the weekend. She'd barely seen him except for the time he'd mowed her grass Saturday evening. They couldn't build a relationship that way.

He looked delicious in a taupe suit and light blue shirt. A fresh tan from that hour of yard work darkened his lean face, and the memory of how he'd looked shirtless and sweaty made her temperature spike.

She rose. His pace faltered again as his hazel eyes roved over her new wraparound dress. She loved the way the fuchsia fabric hugged her breasts and waist and floated just above her knees. But she loved his nostril-flaring reaction even more.

Working primarily from home since she'd left KCL meant she had an extremely limited professional wardrobe. Most of that was too big. She'd spent Sunday afternoon shopping because she needed both work and cruise wear. By the time she'd returned from the outlet mall last night Rand's door had been securely shut. He'd left a note in the kitchen telling her he'd already eaten dinner.

He snapped his head forward and stalked toward his inner sanctum, but not before Tara noted the appreciative expansion of his pupils. Encouraged, she gathered her notepad and followed him.

"We have a ton of stuff to get through before we leave for the cruise on Friday. The first brand's most recent financials are waiting on your desk, and the president and VP are due at eight-thirty."

Four more nights and she'd have him all to herself…along with 2800 people on the ship, that is. She almost danced in her new d'Orsay pumps with anticipation.

Rand stopped so quickly she plowed into his back. His heat and scent enfolded her, but she righted herself and smoothed the spot where her pen had touched his suit coat, checking for a stain. None. Good.

He stiffened and stepped out of reach. "What is that?"

She tracked his gaze and stated the obvious, "A coffee-pot. When you're not using it the roll-down door will conceal it."

He turned his thin-lipped frown from the new addition on the shelving unit to her. "Where did it come from? And why is it here?"

"I picked it up this morning at your favorite coffee shop, along with a pound of freshly ground beans. The pot has a timer. I'll set it up so your coffee will be ready each morning when you arrive, and since you insist on leaving home without breakfast, I'm having it delivered from the KCL cafeteria every day at eight because you're cranky when you're hungry."

Her announcement earned her a darker scowl.

"I've chosen this week's menu, but you're welcome to make adjustments if you like. Here are the chef's suggestions for next week after we return from our cruise. Of course, I didn't tell him why we'd be out of the office since that would defeat the purpose of an incognito inspection."

She offered him the list of choices. When one of his hands

clenched the handles of his leather laptop bag and the other remained fisted by his side, she put the paper in his in-box.

"Tara—"

"You're welcome," she interrupted. She'd learned by his growls that he didn't like her doing things for him such as his laundry or preparing meals and leaving them in the refrigerator. But she had to cook and clean for herself. Doing so for one more wasn't a bother. In fact, after a year of silence and solitude she liked having someone else to look after.

She crossed to the pot and filled a mug, which she then set on his blotter. "I've already dealt with most of your e-mail, but I flagged a couple for your attention. Do you need anything else before you tackle your in-box?"

She could almost hear him grinding his teeth as he opened his bag and withdrew his computer. "No."

"I'll bring in your breakfast as soon as it's brought up, and I'll let you know when the first management team arrives."

She turned on her heel and retreated to her office.

"Tara, it won't work."

She pivoted and examined his hard face. "What won't?"

"Buttering me up."

She frowned. "*Buttering you up* implies I want something."

He closed the distance between them in two long strides, not stopping until he was so close she could see the gleam on his freshly shaven jaw and smell his cologne and a hint of mint toothpaste. "You're after a wedding ring."

Her breath caught and her heart skipped. He didn't know that for sure. He was only guessing. What would he do if she confirmed his suspicions? He couldn't fire her without jeopardizing his part of the will. But he might fortify the walls barricading his heart, and she had a formidable battle on her hands already.

"I'm after a mutually satisfying relationship. That's it."

And it was everything. Five years ago he'd been her playmate and her bedmate. She wanted both back. And she wanted more. Much more.

His intense gaze made her want to squirm, but she'd told nothing but the truth.

"I don't believe you."

"Well…that's certainly honest. My mother always claimed trust was built on actions, not words. So I guess I'll have to prove to you that I'm not after anything that you won't willingly give."

The trick was convincing him to give willingly.

Tara had given Rand space this past week and he'd used it to avoid her. That ended now.

Excitement and anticipation quickened her pulse and dampened her skin late Friday afternoon. She had three nights at sea with Rand to look forward to. Three nights and four days of sharing a cabin. And a bed.

She could hardly wait. The Miami-to-the-Bahamas Rendezvous trip would be her first cruise and her first real vacation in six years, but neither was the main attraction. The man ahead of her held that honor. She wanted to get Rand to relax with her, to leave the world of work, tailored suits and tightly knotted ties behind. His current navy twill pants, white polo shirt and baseball cap were a good start.

She followed him into their assigned cabin, mimicking his moves of inspecting the closet and the tiny lavatory, which contained a sink, toilet and compact shower/bath stall. Definitely not large enough for two.

Reserving a middle-of-the-road cabin—not the cheapest, nor one of the luxury suites—had seemed the best way to blend in. The room was smaller than she'd expected. But then what did she know about cruising? Nothing. And the cabin's limited size could work to her advantage. There was literally nowhere for Rand to hide.

Besides the bed, there was a love seat, two tiny bedside tables and coffee table, as well as a wall unit with drawers, a minifridge and a television quietly playing a show about the proper use of life jackets. Seeing those life jackets in the center of the bed reminded her that she'd soon be out of her depth. In more ways than one.

Rand set his cap on a shelf, snapped off the TV and inspected the narrow rectangular space with his hands on his hips. He crossed the carpet and slid open the glass door. Warm sea-scented air flooded the air-conditioned room. Tara joined him on a private balcony about the size of a single bed and looked over the railing. Lifeboats hung from the sides of the ship just below their balconies.

The theme song from *Titanic* launched in her brain. But even that chilling intrusion couldn't dampen her enthusiasm. She wanted to bounce and giggle. Instead, she trailed Rand back inside. He didn't look happy.

"Is there a problem?"

His gaze landed on the bed they'd soon be sharing before returning to hers. "The room is clean, uncluttered and suitably equipped for the price point. The textiles could be fresher."

He seemed more tense than usual despite his casual attire. "Are you worried about being out of the office? Mitch's PA assured me your brother could handle everything until Tuesday when we return."

"I'm sure he can."

"Rand? Are you okay?"

He looked at her, his gaze running over the flirty strapless apricot sundress that left her shoulders and most of her legs bare. "Why wouldn't I be?"

"You tell me." She tilted her head and her new dangly gold

earrings tapped the sensitive spot on her neck—the one that drove her wild when Rand grazed the skin with his teeth. She couldn't wait for him to do it again, and if this trip went according to plan, he'd do so often.

She'd dreamed about strolling hand in hand on the beaches during the day and on the deck by moonlight, quiet dinners and sharing his bed.

They hadn't been intimate since that night she'd pleasured him. Instead of spending quality time together this past week they'd had an endless series of meetings with the executive staff during the day, and he'd spent evenings in his bedroom working on his laptop. They probably hadn't had two hours total of private face time since Monday morning. That didn't mean she hadn't been aware of his every movement both at home and work.

She was counting on the forced togetherness of the cruise making it impossible for him to keep his distance. "I've never cruised before. I can't wait for you to show me the ropes."

Cruising wouldn't be the only first she'd shared with him, but telling a commitment-phobic man she'd been a virgin before they'd slept together that first night hadn't seemed like a good idea at the time. She was pretty sure the revelation would have ended not only their evening but also their relationship.

His eyes narrowed. "Aren't you the one who claimed the discounted rates made cruising affordable?"

"I've never had anyone to go with." Except him. "My mother was afraid of the water and Nadia wasn't interested." She dug in to her carry-on and pulled out the cruise materials. "We need to sign up for our shore excursions."

His frown deepened. "I'm here to work, not play. You're here as camouflage. You're on your own except for the lifeboat drill and dinners where we'll need to present ourselves as a couple. Do whatever you want. Go ashore. Use the spa. KCL will cover your expenses. *Reasonable* expenses. No jewelry. No designer clothing."

Taken aback by the rapid unraveling of her plans, she struggled to regroup. If she didn't change his mind, their romantic getaway would be a solitary vacation. She'd been alone enough since her mother died. "But…how will you find out the reasons bookings are down if you don't do the full cruise experience?"

"I know what to look for."

"I could help."

"If this is your first cruise, then you won't recognize substandard issues."

He had a point. "You could teach me."

"Tara—"

"What about the welcoming party?"

"I need to check the ship and the chaos of castoff is the best time."

His hard gaze pinned her in place. She scrambled for a valid reason to be with him.

"Do you really want to tip your hand and let them know you're here on our first day? I mean, I realize the check-in associate saw your name, but you had on your hat and your passport still lists a California address. I don't think she recognized you or made the connection to KCL. We should stick together. You said yourself we'll draw less attention as a couple."

His lips thinned in irritation. "Fine. But don't expect to play inseparable newlyweds throughout the cruise."

Newlyweds. The word sent her temperature skyrocketing. Her gaze bounced to the bed, then back to Rand's face. The banked heat in his eyes made her shiver, and the obvious fact that he wanted her kept her going.

She licked her dry lips. She would soon have him exactly

where she wanted him, but could she make him happy to be there? Could she make him yearn to share her bed the way he used to?

That was the mission she intended to accomplish over the next three nights.

Seven

Rand slid his key card into the lock. He'd deliberately stayed out well past midnight to avoid sharing the domesticated get-ready-for-bed routine.

As soon as he crossed the threshold a sense of confinement doubled his pulse rate, constricted his lungs and pushed sweat from his pores. He'd spent months at sea working all over KCL ships and in almost every capacity and slept in cabins barely large enough to turn around in. Three nights of sharing a balcony cabin wouldn't be a problem.

If his roommate were anyone else.

His claustrophobic reaction had nothing to do with the dimensions of the room, and everything to do with the woman he'd left in the bar hours earlier. But even though the comedian onstage had been entertaining, Rand had needed to get away from Tara's laugh. It brought back too many memories—memories of a time when he'd let his guard down.

He eased the door closed and entered the unlit room as silently as possible. Would she be waiting up for him? Or had she gone to bed?

Bed. The heavy throb of his heart echoed a yard lower.

He searched the mattress in the darkness. The white terry-cloth elephant sitting in the center of the spread was the bed's only occupant. Rand had spent nine months between his junior and senior years of college working as a cabin steward. Back then he'd known how to form a dozen different animals from rolled and folded bath towels.

As his eyes adjusted to the lack of light he noted the empty lavatory and his suitcase sitting on the love seat. He stopped in his tracks. Empty bed. Empty chair. No Tara. Another possibility snagged him like a briar ripping along his skin.

The Rendezvous brand primarily targeted couples, but there were always singles on board. Had Tara given up on landing him and lingered in the bar to hook a more willing victim?

An uncomfortable burn settled in his stomach. He scanned the deserted cabin once more. The fluttering bottom corner of the curtain caught his eye and pulled him forward. He pushed back the panel and found Tara sitting on the balcony. She hadn't bothered to turn on the light.

That wasn't relief filling his lungs. The sea air simply made it easier to breathe. He shoved the sliding glass door open the rest of the way. "Seasick?"

She lifted her face. Moonlight washed her cheeks. She'd removed her makeup, but not her dress. From his vantage point above her, the strapless bodice revealed a tempting shadow of cleavage, and then the ocean breeze caught her zigzag hem, drawing his gaze from her sexy sandals to an arousing length of sleek thighs. "No."

"Then why aren't you in bed?"

"I forgot my nightgown."

Her reply hit him like a kick in the crotch, propelling the air from his lungs. Did she think he was stupid enough to fall for that? "How convenient."

She winced at his sarcasm. "Our luggage wasn't delivered until almost nine. By the time I unpacked and realized I'd left my nightie in the dryer, the gift shop had closed. Can I borrow a T-shirt tonight? Unless you don't mind if I sleep naked."

The lower half of his anatomy responded with resounding approval. Luckily, his brain kicked in. Tara had always been good at making her lies sound believable. Too bad he hadn't known that then. But he made a mental note that the luggage had been delivered late. "I'll get a shirt."

She rose. "Thank you."

He backed inside and headed for his luggage. Two flicks later it opened. He withdrew a white T-shirt and handed it over.

"Thanks. I'll only be a minute." Tara crossed the shadowy cabin quickly and disappeared into the bathroom. The door closed.

Something about watching her pad across a bedroom hit him like a double shot of espresso. Sleep would be a long time coming.

Rand eyed the bed and debated stripping to his boxers and getting under the covers before she returned. Stripping…the way Tara was currently on the other side of that wall. He gritted his teeth against another below-the-belt pulse of arousal.

Moments later the door opened. Tara returned, leaving the lavatory light on. Despite the extra-tall size, his shirt only covered her to the tops of her thighs, leaving a mouthwatering amount of leg bare. Even in the moonlight he could make out the shape and jiggle of her breasts beneath the loose white fabric as she hung her dress in the closet. When she turned toward the bed he saw the raised texture of her erect nipples and silently swore.

Was she wearing anything at all under there? Or would he be able to slide his hand beneath the cotton and cup her bare bottom?

You're not cupping anything.

"Which side?" she asked.

It took a few seconds for his brain to engage and figure out she meant which side of the bed. "I don't care."

She picked up the elephant and smiled. "Isn't he adorable?"

"The more creative the animals, the better you'll tip your steward at the end of the voyage."

She stuck her tongue out. "Spoilsport."

The childish gesture reminded him how much fun he'd had with her before she'd betrayed him. Few Florida residents hadn't visited the proliferation of theme parks and tourist traps dotting the state like mushrooms. But oddly enough neither she nor he had. They'd spent a lot of their time visiting amusement parks and acting like kids during the day and igniting the sheets like very naughty adults at night. Screaming on roller-coaster rides or in passion made it easy to avoid personal topics, and playing tourist with Tara had been like having the childhood he and his siblings hadn't had.

She'd been one of the few people he'd been able to relax with.

More fool him.

She carefully set the towel creature on the shelf before lifting the covers on the far side of the bed and climbing between the sheets. "Bathroom's all yours."

Her comment jarred him into action. He retrieved his shaving kit and the essentials and retreated to the head. After brushing his teeth he donned clean boxers and sat on the closed toilet lid. How long would it take her to fall asleep? He gave her ten additional minutes before snapping off the light and easing open the door.

She must have gotten up and closed the curtains. He wanted them open, but didn't want to wake her with the noise.

He couldn't see anything in the pitch-black room, but he could hear Tara's breathing coming slow, even and deep as he approached the bed. He slid between the sheets and lay stiffly, flat on his back. He folded his hands behind his head and stared at the ceiling he could barely make out, dreading the sleepless night ahead. Dreaded lying beside Tara. Wanting her. His sex thickened and ached—a problem any sane man would have handled in the shower.

No, a sane man would take the sex she offered without second thoughts.

But Rand knew how skillfully she'd cast her net last time, how easily she'd suckered him into wanting more than a casual fling despite his vow to never marry, have children or let a woman depend on him.

Tara's breathing altered. She rolled over and snuggled up to him. One silky smooth leg bent and rested on his thigh. Her hand splayed over his sternum. He ground his teeth until his jaw hurt. And then her hand shifted. Downward. Her burning touch skimmed over his bare skin and came to rest just above his navel. His heart slammed against his ribs. Another half inch and she'd encounter the evidence of his horniness, which even now stretched toward her hand.

Was she asleep or playing him? He'd bet his Porsche 911 Carrera S Cabriolet it was the latter.

Why are you denying yourself? She used you last time. It's time for reimbursement. With interest.

Good point.

He wanted her and he'd take what she offered. Forewarned was forearmed, or so the cliché claimed. As for her falling in love with him… Impossible. For that to happen she'd have to be a different kind of woman. One who didn't profess her love for one man and then screw his father days later.

Rand covered her hand with his and guided it lower until

her palm rested over his engorged flesh. The thin knit of his boxers offered no protection from the scalding heat of her touch and his erection jerked in response. A reflex. Nothing more.

Tara's breath hitched. Her fingers twitched, and then tension invaded her lax muscles. Either she'd been asleep and he'd woken her or she was damned good at faking it.

And with Tara Anthony he couldn't trust his judgment to know the difference.

Waking with a handful of Rand was nothing short of a dream or a fantasy.

Tara tried to focus her rousing brain and figure out what was going on. Her fingers curled around thick, cotton-covered steel. Oh, yes. Definitely Rand. She inhaled a shaky breath and his familiar scent confirmed the identification. His palm covered the back of her hand, anchoring it in place.

She tipped back her head, but she couldn't see his features in the inky room. "What—?"

"It's just sex," he rasped in a low, husky voice that made her insides sizzle with sexual excitement.

"Okay." *For now.* She tested his length and his breath hissed.

He rolled her onto her back. One hair-roughened leg separated hers and pinned her in place. His big, hot hand released hers to stroke from her thigh to beneath her borrowed T-shirt. His palm coasted over her panties, her waist and covered her breast. Sure. Fast. Impatient. He found her nipple like a heat-seeking missile and tweaked it until she squirmed with need.

"I won't marry you."

She bit her lip. She hadn't expected winning him back to be easy. But this was a gamble she had to take. A gamble with risks. "I didn't ask you to."

His mouth took hers, his tongue plunged, dueled, stroked.

He devoured her as if his control had snapped, as if he couldn't get enough of her. And that was exactly what she wanted.

She didn't know what had brought on this change of heart, but she wasn't about to argue. She wanted this, wanted Rand. She needed to be consumed by his passion.

She smoothed her hands down the warm supple skin of his back and over his buttocks. The muscles contracted beneath her caress. She dragged her nails back up his spine in a featherlight scrape the way she knew he liked and savored his shudder. He wouldn't react to her touch so easily if he didn't desire her.

He fisted the hem of the T-shirt and ripped it over her head. She wished she could see his face when he looked at her, but she could only sense his eyes on her when he braced himself on one straight arm above her.

His fingers curled over her panties and snatched them past her ankles. That same hand skimmed back up her legs and found her wetness with unwavering accuracy. She started at the electrifying jolt of arousal. He bent and took her nipple into his hot mouth.

His fingers and tongue swirled simultaneously and everything inside her turned liquid, molten. He wasn't gentle, but she didn't want him to be. Pleasure blossomed within her, bowing her back and pouring out of her mouth in a low moan. Tara tangled her fingers in his hair and held him to her breast as relentless waves of pleasure pounded her.

She'd missed this. Missed *him.* His touch, the hungry tugs of his mouth and the steam of his breath on her skin felt so good. Better than anything or anyone she'd tried and failed to find since he'd left her.

The snarling knot of need twisted tighter and tighter, but she wasn't ready to unravel yet, wasn't ready to have this heady hunger satiated. She wanted to savor the rush of sensations, so she fought off her climax. Fought and failed.

Against her will, release snapped through her muscles and whirled through her core, leaving the tickling, tingling sensation in her toes that only Rand could deliver.

Before she could catch her breath he lifted his head. "Where are the condoms?"

With her body still quivering, she rolled to her side and opened the drawer, saying a silent prayer of thanks that she'd been optimistic and prepared. Her fingers closed around a plastic packet. She lay back. He'd removed his briefs and his thick erection strained against her thigh for attention.

Rand took the condom from her, leaving her hands free to map his taut frame as he dealt with the protection. Her senses seemed heightened to his textures, his scent, his heat. She shaped the mounds of his pectorals, thumbed his tiny hard nipples, traced the ridged muscles of his abdomen, his appendix scar, and finally combed her fingers through the tangle of curls at the root of his arousal.

When she reached lower he swore, grabbed her wrists and pinned them to the pillow beside her head. He shifted until his rock-hard thighs spread hers. His thick shaft nudged her entrance. Eager to receive him, Tara lifted her hips and Rand slid deep in one long, slow thrust. He felt so right buried deep inside her, as if a missing part had finally been found and returned.

The darkness intensified the sounds of his harsh breathing, the feel of his hard, hot body plunging into hers again and again, and the unique aroma of his skin and their sex. Wanting to touch him, she struggled against the hands holding her captive, but Rand held fast.

His back arched. He found her mouth for one brief, voracious, breath-stealing kiss and then his mouth grazed her jaw. He nipped her earlobe, her neck. Each gentle love bite shot bolts of desire straight to her core, arousing her more than she'd ever thought possible. She nuzzled his temple, his brow.

"Rand, please," she begged and struggled to free her hands. She needed to hold him, to pleasure him the way he did her, to show him how good this was. How good *they* were. Together. This wasn't just sex. It was tenderness and sharing.

He answered by shifting both of her hands to one of his. His weight held her in place as his other hand shifted to her breast. He buffed her distended flesh with his thumb, sparking a response deep inside her, and then he bisected her breasts, her belly and found her center. He plied her with precision until her breaths came in pants and her muscles knotted. Orgasm whipped through her once more, causing her body to spasm and his name to explode from her lips.

He muffled his answering growl against her neck, sending the vibration straight down her spine. And then he stilled above her except for the bellows of his chest pressing and withdrawing from hers. The cabin fell silent except for their gasping breaths and the thunder of her pulse in her ears.

He released her hands, but before she could wrap her arms around him he slid to her side and rolled onto his back, throwing a forearm across his face.

Satisfaction engulfed her. *This* was what they used to share. *This* is what she'd missed when he said goodbye. *This* is why she couldn't sleep with Everett.

Because she still loved Rand.

She twisted to her side and laid a palm on his sweat-slick chest over the whorls of hair covering his racing heart, then she leaned in to press a kiss to his skin.

He stiffened and bolted upright, dodging her lips and dislodging her hand. He rose and headed for the bathroom. The door closed and the lock clicked, dimming her rosy glow. The shower turned on and her euphoria sank like an anchor.

That was not how she'd wanted their evening to end.

She may have taken a giant step forward in having him want to make love to her, but she'd taken two steps back. He'd literally locked her out.

Fun for one just didn't have the same kick as sharing new experiences.

Tara turned in her snorkeling gear, gathered her towel and beach bag and trudged barefoot through the sand between the cabanas selling drinks, souvenirs and beach supplies toward the barbecue area of Crescent Key, Kincaid Cruise Line's tiny private island and the cruise's first stop.

She would have enjoyed exploring the brightly colored reef and fish so much more with Rand by her side. But he'd been gone when she'd awoken this morning. After years of listening for her mother, Tara had considered herself a light sleeper, but apparently she wasn't easily roused after two off-the-Richter-scale orgasms. She'd never heard Rand get up or leave.

"Hey, are you solo?" a blond guy about Tara's age called out as he jogged up beside her. He was good-looking in a toothy, preppy kind of way.

"Yes." Not by choice.

"Me, too. I'm Joe. I was in your snorkeling group."

She hadn't noticed. "I'm Tara."

"Where are you headed next?"

"Lunch and then the Jet Ski Zone. I have a couple of hours before my lesson."

"Same here. Mind if I tag along?"

She wished Rand would look at her with the kind of interest Joe showed. But Rand might not even see the new bikini she'd bought with him in mind. And she didn't want to give Joe the wrong idea. "I don't think—"

He held up his hands and backed a step. "Not putting the moves on you or anything. Unless you're interested, that is.

It's just that this place is really geared for couples, and my travel buddies have split. We were supposed to meet for lunch, but I haven't spotted them yet."

"I'm with someone. He stayed onboard." And then an idea hit her. "Travel buddies?"

"There are six of us in three cabins. We were fraternity brothers at UVA, and we've met every summer since gradua-tion for a cruise vacation. This is our fifth." He nodded to someone behind her. Tara turned and saw another guy about the same age headed in their direction. He wore the same kind of overlong swim trunks—board shorts, she'd heard them called.

"Is that one of your friends?"

"Yeah."

"This is my first cruise, and I have a lot to learn. Would you and your friends be willing to answer a few questions over lunch? I'll buy the first round of drinks."

"You've got yourself a deal, Tara."

Tara had lied. But the question was, when?

Rand strode through the sand, searching left and right for Tara. Had she lied when she said she loved him? Or lied when she said she didn't?

Because last night she'd made love like she meant it.

He hadn't seen it in her eyes. But he'd felt it in her touch. Tasted it in her kiss. Heard it in the way she sighed his name.

Like she had before she'd betrayed him.

Was it a betrayal?

She'd said she loved him.

But you dumped her and told her to find another man— one who could give her what she needed.

But not his father. Anybody but him. She'd known how much Everett Kincaid liked to stick it to his oldest son.

Or had she? Rand's gait faltered. He couldn't remember discussing his strained relationship with his father with her.

You're making excuses for her.

Damn. Damn. Damn. She'd gotten to him. Again.

But if she was starting to care about him, then he had to nip those feelings in the bud. Before it was too late. He couldn't afford to let Tara get close or convince herself she loved him, because he couldn't live with another woman's death or near-death on his conscience.

Cursing his weakness for Tara and his stupidity for craving her body and her company, he scanned the cabanas, beaches and tables. How hard could it be to find one curly-haired blonde on a small island with no roads and no exit other than the tender that had brought her over? Crescent Key had been named for its shape. KCL had posted different excursion sites in and around the island. If he followed the curve long enough he'd find Tara.

The hot sand seeped into his sandals and the sun toasted his bare back. He'd dressed in swim trunks—like a tourist—as camouflage, but it had been a long time since he'd been comfortable in such casual clothing. Five years, to be exact. He'd spent every day since leaving Miami trying to get Wayfarer Cruise Lines ahead of KCL.

Trying to beat Everett Kincaid at his own game.

A laugh stopped Rand in his tracks. Tara's laugh. He pivoted and followed the sound around a tiki-hut bar and found her at an umbrella-covered table surrounded by a group of six guys. Twenty-somethings. Closer to her age than Rand's thirty-five. Empty plates, beer bottles, drink cups and a couple of half-filled bowls of chips and salsa littered the picnic table.

The burn in his gut caught him off guard. Indigestion? Probably. He'd speak to the ship's chef.

Or was he jealous? Couldn't be. To be jealous he'd have to have feelings for Tara beyond the anger that festered inside him at her manipulativeness. Feelings beyond the respect for her work. Beyond lust for her body.

Her black bikini left her back almost completely bare.

"Tara."

She startled at the bark of her name and twisted around on the bench seat. "Rand. Hi."

Was that a guilty flush on her cheeks? Could she be auditioning potential lovers when she'd left his bed only hours ago?

He planted a hand on her shoulder and nodded to her male harem. "Gentlemen. Rand Kincaid. Kincaid Cruise Lines. I hope you don't mind if I steal my assistant."

It wasn't a question.

He noted Tara's widened eyes, and then one of the guys laughed and grinned at Tara. "You work for the cruise line? That explains all the questions."

Tara's shoulder shrugged beneath Rand's hand. He looked down to see her nose—now sporting a fresh dusting of freckles—wrinkle. "Sorry for the secrecy. But it really is my first cruise, and I know very little about what's out there. I appreciate you giving me your thoughts on the comparisons between KCL vacations and our competitors'."

She tucked a pen into the spirals of a little pink notebook. Rand recalled Tara had always carried a notebook in her purse. She was a big fan of note taking. Had been even back when she'd worked for his father. A breeze ruffled the pages—pages filled with her small neat handwriting. Handwriting not formatted like addresses or phone numbers.

Working? She'd been *working?* Didn't she realize each of these guys eyed her as if she were a tender and juicy filet mignon and they couldn't wait to take a bite? And given the mouthwatering cleavage he could see from his position above her, Rand couldn't blame them.

She rose and gathered her belongings. He let his hand fall from her shoulder.

"I guess this means you'll have to skip your first Jet Ski ride," one of the guys said and scowled at Rand. "That sucks. She wanted to learn."

Tara bit her lip, and disappointment flashed across her face. "I guess so. But I am supposed to be working. It was nice meeting you. Thanks again for your help."

"Thanks for the drinks," a blond guy replied. "Maybe we'll see you at the luau tonight. Save a dance for me."

"I'll see what I can do, Joe." Tara waved and looked questioningly at Rand.

He grasped her elbow and led her to the opposite side of the tiki hut from the devouring eyes of her fan club. "You were working?"

"Yes, and I have some really good info for you. But why did you blow your cover?"

Good question. He didn't like the answer. He *had* been jealous. Dammit. More fool him. "You've never ridden a Jet Ski?"

"No."

A smart man would head back to the ship and put some clothes on the woman. His gaze raked over her lightly tanned skin, savoring the swell of her breasts in the bikini top, the curve of her waist and the dip of her navel above a tiny skirted bottom. And then there were her legs.

The rush of blood to his groin annoyed the hell out of him. He grabbed her hand and towed her behind him. "Let's go."

"The boat's the other way."

"Ship," he corrected automatically. "But the Jet Skis are this way."

"But—"

"You want lessons. You'll get lessons. From me." And he'd be damned if she'd be dancing with the frat boy later.

Eight

The hard thighs clamped around Tara's and the firm hands grasping her ribs just below her breasts should have made her feel relaxed and comfortable. But they had the opposite effect.

She held her breath as the Jet Ski shot over the crest of a wave and splashed down again. Exhilaration made her pulse race, intensifying her other senses to the tang of salt on her lips, the warmth of the sun on her skin and the tease of wind in her hair. The vibration of the machine beneath her and the feel of the man behind her made her…well, hot in a way that the sea water spraying over her skin couldn't cool.

A horn sounded, signaling the end of their hour on the personal watercraft. Disappointment sagged through her. She wasn't ready to go in, wasn't ready to share the man or the machine with other people on the tiny island or go back to work. She could happily ride for hours longer in the aquamarine-blue water with Rand's arms and legs wrapped around her.

As if he sensed her reluctance to return Rand transferred his hands from her torso to flank hers on the handlebars. She instantly missed the heat of his palms. He throttled them down and made a wide U-turn toward shore. She couldn't believe he'd let her drive, but he'd insisted she learn.

She leaned back against him to catch her breath. Despite the life jackets separating their bodies, she couldn't be more conscious of every hard, muscular inch of him behind her and the strong arms bracketing her.

"That was fun," she shouted over the engine's rumble as she tilted her head back onto his shoulder. "And we survived without Jaws coming up to eat us."

"You're not out of the water yet," Rand growled in her ear, then sank his teeth into her neck in a love bite.

She squealed and squirmed then twisted on the wide, cushioned seat she straddled to look at Rand. The wicked grin on his tanned face made her breath hitch and her heart squeeze. *This* was the man she'd fallen in love with. The one who played as hard as he worked.

Her laughter died and her smile wobbled. "Thank you. That was great."

His smile faded and tension invaded his features. Her reflection stared back at her from his mirrored sunglasses, but she'd bet if she could see his eyes, she'd see the barriers drop back in place, as well. "You're welcome."

He guided the craft into the cove, where they would be anchored for the next group, and fell in line behind a dozen other riders.

She faced forward again and burrowed deeper into the arms surrounding her. "But you really blew your cover when you flashed your KCL ID and commandeered a ride when you weren't registered for the excursion."

He shrugged against her back. "The attendant probably

won't talk to anyone on the ship, but it doesn't matter if he does. I've seen what I needed to see."

Her breath snagged. Did that mean they'd leave the cruise early? She didn't want to fly back to Miami from Nassau tomorrow. She wasn't ready. She wanted her three nights. "Like what?"

"That's strictly need-to-know information."

She bristled. "We're a team. You said so."

"And KCL is an information sieve."

"I'm not part of the gossip mill. I never was."

An employee came forward to anchor their ride, temporarily stilling her protest. Rand climbed off and waded toward shore. Tara followed, collected her beach bag and towel and stomped after him. He led her to the closest bar and bought a couple of bottles of water using his cruise ID/charge card/room key.

Glancing longingly at an unoccupied hammock as they passed, Tara followed him toward an empty pair of lounge chairs tucked beneath a shade tree. She dumped her stuff beside the chair and sat. Maybe she could nap in a hammock later. The ship wouldn't sail until after tonight's luau. They had hours left on the island. Unless Rand had a helicopter swoop in and take them home. She knew Everett had sometimes done that because she'd arranged the flights.

She accepted the bottle he offered. "Rand, how can I help you if you keep me out of the loop?"

He glanced pointedly at the guests in nearby chairs. "You can help by remembering this is a confidential investigation."

His abrupt tone made her hackles rise. She gritted her teeth and sipped her water. Trust. It all went back to trust—or the lack thereof. She hadn't earned his. Yet. But she would.

She set her water aside and dug a bottle of sunscreen out of her bag. She'd been good about slathering it on, but her fair skin could only handle so much sun and most of the excursion activities were held out in the open. The cloudless cerulean skies might be good for business, but not for her pale complexion. Rand, on the other hand, had already darkened several shades.

The urge to press herself against his warm, tanned skin gnawed at her. "I don't suppose I can talk you in to hula lessons later?"

"If you insist." No smile accompanied his words. The fun, playful guy had vanished. Rand set his water on the table between them and rose. He snatched the lotion bottle out of her hands and made a circular motion with one finger. Tara turned her back. A shiver she couldn't suppress rippled over her in anticipation of his hands on her skin.

Rand straddled the chaise behind her. His legs flanked hers as they had on the Jet Ski, but this time without touching. She regretted the scant distance.

She heard the snick of the cap, smelled the coconut-scented sunscreen and then his hands settled on her shoulders. The lotion was cool, but his hands quickly warmed the cream *and her* as he slicked it over her back, arms and shoulders.

His fingers dipped beneath the edge of her bikini bottom just above her buttocks and her breath stalled then quickened. He dragged a finger along the elastic. "You're burning here."

Her breasts tightened and her core heated. She considered leaning back against his chest so he could reach her front, but the other sun-worshippers were too close. Instead, she gave in to the temptation to stroke his hot sun-baked, bare thighs. The wiry hairs tickled her palms and his muscles turned rock-hard beneath her hands.

He caught her wrists and returned her hands to her lap, then dropped the sunscreen bottle between her legs. Disappointment slid through her.

"You can do the rest." His voice sounded huskier than usual.

She twisted to look at his face, but he rose and stalked back to his chair. He was always putting distance between them. However, the ridge in his trunks as he eased onto the lounger told her what she needed to know. Touching her hadn't left him unaffected. Good.

She was tempted to suggest they return to the ship and the privacy of their cabin to try and alleviate their mutual hunger, but she'd seen a side of Rand today that she'd begun to fear had vanished forever. She was determined to lure the fun-loving man out again.

"Want me to do your back?" Her palms tingled in antici-pation.

"No." That hard, bitten-off response carried the sting of re-jection, but she'd made too much progress in the past hour to give up so easily.

"I bet you know all the good hiding places on the island," she prompted.

He gulped his water instead of replying.

"We could find one."

She couldn't see behind his glasses, but his sudden still-ness, the flare of his nostrils and the thin white line forming around his mouth was hard to miss. "You're the one who said we have a confidence issue with KCL employees. Getting caught banging my PA in the lighthouse won't improve it."

She flinched at the crude statement, but acknowledged he had a point. Her gaze shifted to the black-and-white diamond-patterned lighthouse looming over the island. Too bad. She would have liked a private tour of the tall structure…and anything else Rand had to offer behind the thick, sturdy walls.

Forcing her eyes back to Rand she decided to aim for a less sensitive subject. "It must have been fun having an island as a playground when you were growing up. Did you and Nadia and Mitch come here often?"

"It wasn't a playground. When we came, we came to work."

"Doing what?" Other than telling her he'd worked onboard several ships, he'd never given her details.

"Mitch worked watercraft. Jet Skis, parasailing. Nadia taught snorkeling and kayaking."

She waited for him to expand. He didn't. "What did you do?"

"Food prep. Trash detail. Maintenance. Dad always gave me the hottest, dirtiest jobs. The only time I had a job with tips was when I worked as a cabin steward. He liked the idea of me cleaning toilets."

That didn't sound like the Everett she'd known. "Why would he do that?"

"He said if I wanted to run KCL I needed to have an intimate knowledge of the underbelly. He did his best to make sure I got it."

Rand's bitterness brought a lump to her throat. "I'm sorry."

His lips compressed even more. "I'm not. I understand my workforce the way few CEOs do. My father did his best to break me, but in the end he did me a favor."

Tara stared aghast. She'd known Everett could be ruthless with his competitors. But had he been as merciless with his own children? Apparently so.

How could the man Rand described be the same one who'd treated her so well? Had she been so blinded by the excitement of being transferred to the top floor that she'd seen everything through rose-colored glasses?

Maybe even her relationship with Rand.

Doubts made her stomach churn.

No. No. She had loved Rand.

Hadn't she?

Although she had to admit, she'd learned more about him

in the past ten days than she'd learned in the months they'd known each other before. Rand Kincaid was far more complex than the gorgeous, charming guy who'd swept her off her feet, shown her a good time and taught her about the pleasures of sex. But she knew now he'd barely let her scratch the surface.

Shaking her head, she lay back on her chair and pulled the brim of her hat over her face. How could she have believed herself in love with a man she'd barely known?

Because *this* Rand had depth and character and integrity that the younger man she remembered had never displayed.

And he was much more attractive.

"Must be nice to get a paid vacation less than two weeks after starting a new job."

Mitch's bitter comment pulled Tara's attention away from the papers spewing out of the printer Monday afternoon. She swiveled her desk chair and saw him entering her office with a long, confident stride very similar to his brother's.

She'd never had a problem with Mitch when she worked for KCL last time. In fact, she'd considered him the peace-maker in many of the disagreements between Rand and Everett. But ever since she'd returned he'd been cool.

"Back off, Mitch," Rand said from his open door before Tara could reply. "If you have a problem with the way my staff or I operate, then you come to me."

The brothers faced off, each with his hands clenched by his sides. Their stances and profiles were so similar. They shared the same tall frames, broad shoulders, thick dark brows, straight noses and stubborn chins. Tara had never noticed the similarities before.

"You skipped out without saying a word." Mitch's voice carried an undercurrent Tara couldn't fathom.

"Your PA knew we were going out of town, and she

knew when we'd be back. If she didn't inform you, that's your problem."

"She didn't know where you'd gone and you didn't answer your cell phone. Hell, for all I knew you'd headed back to California." He and Rand exchanged another long, silent look.

"I was out of cell range."

"A vacation violates the terms of the will."

"Then it's a good thing Tara and I weren't on vacation. We were working on KCL business," Rand said in a lowered tone. "I couldn't reveal our plans without raising a flag."

Any remnants of the man who'd shared her cabin and her bed each night of the cruise had vanished the moment they'd stepped ashore this morning.

Rand had indeed danced with her at the luau and made love to her every night of the cruise, but it was as if he didn't want to make love, yet couldn't help himself. And as he'd stated at the beginning of their agreement, he hadn't held her afterward or played happy couple. Each time he'd risen from the bed immediately after his climax, even before their breathing slowed or the sweat dried on their skin. He'd retreated to the bathroom, then returned to lie on his side of the mattress.

The contradiction between mind-melting passion and the detached man on the opposite side of the bed had been disconcerting to say the least. They'd been together. But apart. Far, far apart.

Once they'd reached her home he'd barely allowed them time to drop off their luggage and change into work clothes before heading into the office. He was all business this afternoon, from his tightly knotted navy tie to his polished cognac-colored wingtips. She wasn't sure if she should consider today's carpooling as a sign of progress or just a way for him to guarantee she'd be at her desk and ready to work when he needed something from her. Like the data she'd printed out.

"What were you working on that you couldn't do it here?" Mitch asked.

Rand glanced at Tara. "Have the switchboard pick up the calls and bring your notebook and the spreadsheets into my office."

He turned on his heel and headed for the inner sanctum, closely followed by Mitch. "Dammit, Rand, what's going on?"

Surprised, but happy to be included after he'd shut her out on the island, Tara did as Rand instructed and joined them. She needed a machete to cut through the tense silence in the room.

"Close the door," Rand ordered and Tara did. He jerked his head, indicating she sit in the visitor chair beside Mitch's. "We took a three-night trip on the *Abalone*. Tell him what you found, Tara."

"Whoa. Hold it. You voluntarily went on a cruise? You hate cruising."

Tara's shocked gaze shot from Mitch's to Rand's face. Rand hated cruising? He'd never said anything. And how could he hate traveling on a ship with as much experience as he'd had?

"Necessity." He nodded for Tara to go ahead.

Smothering the questions bouncing around her brain, she flipped open her notebook. "I interviewed about three dozen customers while onboard, but a group of six men who've taken five different destination cruises with Rendezvous over the past five years gave me the most information. They're single, but fit the target age and income demographic of the brand. They said in the past two years the quality and quantity of the food had dropped off noticeably, and the alcoholic drinks appeared to be watered down. They're seriously considering switching to another cruise line for next year's trip."

Rand extended his hand. Tara passed him the spreadsheets. One tanned finger skated down the columns and then stopped. "Two years ago Rendezvous requested and received four-point-six million for refurbishing. From what I saw onboard, none of the textiles has been replaced in ten years. The carpets, drapes and bedspreads are worn and faded. The towels are thin. Not threadbare, but close. I saw chipped dishes in the stacks every time I ate at one of the buffets."

The boat was shabbily decorated? That's what he hadn't wanted to tell her?

His hazel gaze drilled Mitch. "Where did that money go if not into the ships?"

"I have no clue without checking the ledgers."

"Tara will access those for us and print copies. I want you to go over them with a magnifying glass *at home*. I'll do the same. And we need to check every other ship in the brand, because the *Abalone* sure as hell hasn't been refurbished."

Mitch's eyes narrowed. "You think someone is skimming?"

Tara's stomach plunged. Rand suspected embezzlement. And he thought she'd tell the guilty party? Why would he think…

Because you told him you'd lied.

But he'd decided to trust her now. That's what mattered.

Rand's gaze shifted to Tara then back to his brother. "Until we see the other ships and the books I won't know for sure. But it looks that way. And you can thank Tara for pointing us in the right direction. If she hadn't targeted the repeat customers with her questions, we'd never have known where to start looking."

Pleasure and pride bloomed inside her at his praise.

Rand gave her another long, intense look. "This conversation stays in this room. Mitch, I don't even want your PA to get a whiff of it. Not with the way the KCL gossip factory works. If someone is embezzling from KCL, then we don't want to tip them off and give them time to abscond or cover their tracks."

Mitch leaned forward, bracing his elbows on the arms of the chair. "What's the plan?"

"I want every Rendezvous ship inspected for improvements as it comes to port. Since each cruise originates in Miami that's something we can handle without fanfare."

Mitch nodded.

"And with Nadia in Dallas, that means you and I will have to do the legwork because I'm not trusting this to anyone else."

Tara jotted notes and reminders to reschedule appointments set around docking times. She glanced at Rand. "You might want to spot-check the other brands, as well, to cover your investigation."

Both men's gazes focused on her. She shrugged. "My mother loved mysteries. I read a lot of them to her when she was…ill. There were always red herrings to keep from giving away the true villain."

Rand nodded. "Good point, Tara."

She basked in his approval.

"You have to love the devious way a woman's mind works," Mitch added. Tara fought a wince at the jab, and Rand scowled at him.

"Can we have a minute?" Mitch asked Rand and tilted his head toward Tara.

Rand suspected he knew where his brother's train of thought was headed, but he had to hear him out. "Sure. Tara, would you get me a list of the ships' arrival times and dates for the next quarter?"

Mitch didn't speak again until after the door closed behind Tara. "You're trusting *her*?"

After what he'd revealed to Mitch two weeks ago, Rand understood his brother's skepticism. "In this, I am."

"Man, you're screwing her again, aren't you? Are you in love with her again, too?"

The muscles in Rand's back snapped tight. "I was never in love with Tara."

"Bull. Last time Nadia and I took bets on how long you would hold out before you decided to risk the Kincaid Curse and marry the woman."

Rand rose and paced to the window. He stared out at the port, at all that open space but the sense of confinement remained. "Do I look that stupid? Loving a Kincaid is bad news. Besides our parents' lousy marriage, neither you, Nadia or I have had one good relationship between us."

"Nadia came close."

Hands on his hips, he faced his brother. "Yeah, and that turned out great. Her husband and the baby she carried were killed leaving the wedding reception. Have you talked to her?"

"No. I keep meaning to call."

"I'll call her tonight. Tell her what's going on. See if she has any input."

"Terms of the will say she can't work."

"What kind of crazy, manipulative crap is that? She has to stay unemployed and house-sit for a year?"

Mitch shrugged. "Dad wasn't crazy, Rand, despite what you think. And after his first stroke—"

Shock rippled over him. "Stroke? What stroke?"

"The one he had eleven months ago. It was mild. The doctors fixed him up with some clot-busting miracle drug, and he had almost no lingering effects. Didn't even miss a day of work."

"Why didn't you call me?"

"He ordered us not to. He wanted you to come back on your own."

"Crawl back, you mean." Even when facing death his father hadn't wanted him around. Nice to know.

Mitch shook his head. "Believe it or not, I think he respected you more for leaving than he would have if you'd stayed. He kept tabs on Wayfarer. And you."

The claustrophobic sensation intensified. "He should have kept tabs on Rendezvous."

"As CFO, that was my job."

"You don't have access to the full scope of paperwork. The CEO's office does. But we both know Dad was never a hands-on manager. We will get to the bottom of this, Mitch. If I accomplish nothing else this year, I will straighten out the mess he left behind."

"Just don't make a bigger one of your own with your PA. And for godsakes don't knock her up like Dad did that Corbin woman."

"I won't. Fifty more weeks, and then Tara and I are done."

Never mind that Tara brought him more satisfaction in bed and out than any other woman. Their relationship was about sex. Nothing more. Nothing less.

And it was temporary. He couldn't let it be anything else.

"Take a break." Rand's voice interrupted Tara's concentration.

"What?"

"That's the third time you've massaged your neck in the last ten minutes."

She lowered her hand to the kitchen table where they'd spread the Rendezvous data she'd printed out and blinked her gritty eyes. Hours of poring over columns of numbers had given her a headache, and it was getting more difficult to focus. "Sorry."

"It's tedious, mind-numbing work and we're both tired." He stood and stretched, mesmerizing Tara with his lithe, powerful body.

Arousal and renewed energy rushed through her. "I'll make coffee."

"No. It's late. We need to go to bed. This can wait until tomorrow." He turned and walked into the den.

Tara rose on surprisingly unsteady legs. Would he sleep with her tonight? Onboard the ship Rand had shared her bed because he had to. Here he had his own room. Should she invite and/or entice him? Or see what happened?

The old Tara would have waited for him to make the first move. What would the new Tara do?

"Is this your mother?" he called from the den before she could make a decision or formulate a plan.

Tara joined him. He held the picture from the mantel in his hand. "Yes."

"You have her hair."

She reached up self-consciously and touched a curl that had slipped free from her tightly pulled-back style. "No. She has mine. I had it cut and made into a wig for her."

His head snapped in her direction. He searched her hair and face through narrowed eyes. "You can do that?"

"Yes. There are several companies that make custom wigs. It's not cheap, but it was worth every penny. It made her less self-conscious about going out after she lost her hair."

"She had chemotherapy?"

Her throat clogged. She nodded. "Several courses. It was brutal."

He replaced the frame without taking his gaze from hers. "When did you find out?"

"About?"

"Her diagnosis."

"Twenty days after you left for Europe."

His jaw shifted. "And you told my father."

"I— Yes. I couldn't help it…I kind of lost it one day in the office." Embarrassment warmed her cheeks.

"The bastard," Rand spat out. He pivoted sharply and paced to stand at the window overlooking the backyard. She hadn't drawn the curtains yet and fireflies flickered in the darkness.

Rand's spine looked as straight and rigid as steel. His hands fisted and released by his side.

"What do you mean?"

He turned and she caught her breath at the suppressed fury in his eyes. "My father's forte was finding a woman's weak spot and exploiting it."

"I don't think that's what he—"

He closed the distance between them in three swift strides, caught her shoulders and gave her a gentle shake. "Open your eyes, dammit. He was a sorry, no good, conniving son of a bitch. And you are too smart to be this stupid about him."

Tara reeled back at his vehemence. She'd never seen Rand this furious or out of control. "I—I only know what I saw and how Everett treated me."

Her reply seemed to anger him further. His jaw muscles bunched and his lips disappeared into a thin line. He released her and backed away. "I have to make a call. Good night."

He pivoted and left the room. She listened to him ascend the stairs, then his door thumped shut. That answered her question about whether they'd sleep together tonight.

Her thoughts whirred crazily. Her last encounter with Rand five years ago tumbled through her head. *The joke's on dear ol' Dad. He wants you because he thinks I do.*

Was Rand right, or was his view colored by his bitterness toward Everett? Surely Everett wouldn't have used her to score one on Rand? But father and son had been extremely competitive.

On autopilot, Tara returned to the kitchen, piled the Rendezvous reports into a neat stack and slid them into a manila envelope, but making order of the papers did nothing toward organizing her thoughts. She sank into a chair and propped her forehead on her palms.

She hated that everything she'd learned since Rand's return made her question her judgment. Before Rand had come back into her life she'd known right from wrong. Her mother had died. It was Tara's fault. She'd stood by and done nothing when a potential life-saving solution had been offered.

But now...now she didn't know what to think. About her former boss. About her own intelligence.

What had Rand said in the cafeteria that day? Something about Everett never doing anything out of the goodness of his heart and always having a price tag attached. Was it true?

She replayed her last encounter with Everett, searching for clues she'd missed.

Rand will never marry you, my dear. He won't come back for you or help you through this. Let me help, Tara. Let me make everything all right. I'll hire the best oncologists money can buy. Your mother will have top-notch medical care, and I promise, together you and I will minimize her suffering as much as possible.

All I ask in return is that you move in to Kincaid Manor. I need a hostess and a partner. I'm lonely, Tara. But I won't risk all I've worked for, all I've created in building Kincaid Cruise Lines, by marrying again. We are a good team at work, and we can be on a personal level, as well.

I swear I'll stand by you throughout this ordeal. Tara, let me take care of you. Let me take care of everything.

His concern had sounded genuine, and his confession of loneliness had been touching. He'd made his proposition sound so simple and attractive. She'd been surprised but also shamelessly tempted. Not because she was attracted to Everett, but because she'd liked and respected him and believed he wouldn't hurt her already damaged heart even more.

And it wasn't as if she were a shy virgin looking for a man to replace Rand. In fact, she'd sworn off falling in love again.

Everett was only asking for sex and companionship. For her mother's sake Tara should have been able to deliver both.

While she'd debated Everett had draped an arm around her shoulders and pulled her into a fatherly embrace. She'd needed to lean on someone so badly that she hadn't pulled away. Overwhelmed and afraid, she'd wanted to let him take care of everything, and she'd finally whispered okay.

Everett had kissed her on the forehead, on the temple and then on the mouth. She'd held it together until he'd touched her, and then she'd shuddered not with passion but in revulsion. And she'd pushed him away.

Rand had left her, but even if she'd never see him again, the idea of becoming intimate with his father when she'd still loved Rand had made her want to throw up.

In a flash of insight, she'd discovered her Achilles' heel. She'd believed herself willing to do anything to save her mother. But she'd been wrong. She selfishly clung to the only thing of value she had left. Her body. And her mother had paid the price.

If Rand couldn't forgive her for turning to his father, then he'd never forgive her for standing by and letting her mother die. Rand Kincaid respected strength and he abhorred weakness. Sleeping with her proved he'd go to any lengths for the ones he loved.

And Tara had let her mother down.

Nine

Would a selfish bitch cut her hair and have it made into a wig for her mother?

It's just hair. It grows back.

But hadn't Nadia freaked when she'd come out of her coma after the accident and discovered the doctor had shaved her head for brain surgery?

Logical or not, women were possessive of their hair.

But Tara hadn't been.

Rand snapped his cell phone closed when Nadia didn't answer, and turned to stare at his closed bedroom door.

Tara Anthony confused him. The evidence didn't add up.

Would a mercenary tramp take a job far below her salary level and qualifications to stay home and nurse her ailing parent? Tara was too smart to waste her brain in a third-rate small business. From the belated update he'd had her add to her personnel file he knew she must have been bored out of her mind with her previous job.

And yet she'd stuck it out for years.

Would a gold digger stick around for Mitch's and Nadia's sakes when he, Rand admitted, had been an ass? He'd be the first to acknowledge that between his anger toward his father and Tara, his frustration over the tension with Mitch and his worry over his sister and KCL, he'd been a lousy boss. His Wayfarer PA would have been horrified by his behavior. And she would have quit. On the first day. But Tara had put up with his bad attitude.

The Tara he'd known before would have retreated when he barked. She would have left him alone when he hurled insults. But his distancing techniques had failed. This new Tara stood her ground.

Five years ago she'd been a pretty face, a good time. Today she had a new strength and insight he couldn't help but admire. Had her trials with her mother brought about the change?

Had she fooled him with an innocent act five years ago and this backbone of steel was her true character? Or was she fooling him now?

Proof Rand had seen with his own eyes labeled her a gold digger. She'd been coming out of his father's bedroom late at night and had a fresh hickey on her neck, dammit. The buttons of her shirt had been misaligned, which meant at some point they had been unbuttoned.

Why sleep with his father if not for financial gain? Yes, Tara genuinely seemed to have admired his father. *How could any woman be that naive?* But surely her feelings couldn't have run deeper for a man who'd been twice her age? Not unless she'd been looking for a father figure since her father was nowhere to be found.

Her current bargain of shacking up, plus an exorbitant

salary, reinforced the money angle. Could she be hedging her bets? Trying to hook a rich husband but filling her coffers in case she failed to snag him?

Did she really intend to use her salary to pay off her mother's medical bills? Judging by the worn furnishing of the house and her old car and clothing, she certainly wasn't wasting her money on luxuries.

He shoved a hand through his hair in frustration and paced in front of the window. He didn't have the answers and not knowing frustrated the hell out of him.

Just like the Rendezvous books, something in this scenario didn't add up. Something was off-kilter and he couldn't put his finger on what.

Had he made a mistake? Had he misjudged Tara?

If so, when? Then? Or now?

Since he'd moved in Tara had worked as long and hard as he did—longer actually, because she'd done his laundry and cooked for him, despite his demands that she not. In fact, she'd done everything she could to make him comfortable both here and at the office, and he'd given nothing in return except rude remarks, a hard time and mechanical sex.

Even mechanical sex is good with Tara.

He shut down that thought, ignored the involuntary leap of his pulse and stared at the blackened panes.

She mowed her own grass, for godsakes, and had refused his offers to hire a landscaping crew and a housekeeper. If she were looking for Easy Street, she should have jumped on both offers.

Was it all a ruse to lure him into her snare?

As Rand had told Tara downstairs his father specialized in exploiting weaknesses. Could that be what happened? Had his father swooped in on Tara and taken advantage when she didn't stand a chance of resisting? It was beginning to look that way.

A naive girl, as Rand had believed Tara to be five years ago, wouldn't stand a chance against a master manipulator like Everett Kincaid.

Maybe Tara wasn't a greedy fortune hunter.

Maybe she'd been as much of a victim of his father's machinations as the rest of them.

Yeah, and maybe she's taking you for a ride.

Rand's gut told him to trust the earnestness and the pain he saw in those big, blue eyes. And his gut wasn't often wrong. But the consequences of misjudging were too high. For him. For KCL. For Tara.

It all boiled down to whether or not he could forgive her for sleeping with the enemy.

And tonight, that answer was no.

One of them had misjudged Everett. The question was, who?

And the only way Tara could find out was to get to know Rand on a deeper level than the superficial one he'd offered her five years ago. Even if that meant tracking Rand down and battering in the doors he kept closing in her face.

Rand surfaced in the shallow end of the Olympic-size pool located in the health club on the first floor of KCL. His chest rose and fell rapidly from his exertions. Water plastered his dark hair to his skull and streamed down his body like a lover's caress. With his eyes still closed he shook his head, slinging water across her legs.

"Why do you hate cruising?"

His eyes flew open then narrowed. He swiped a hand down his face. She'd been in a chair poolside for the past twenty minutes, watching the sole occupant of the pool slice through the water at a punishing pace, but he must not have noticed. "You're early."

"I thought you'd come in to get started on the Rendezvous requisition lists before any of the other employees arrived. I came in to pull them up for you. When I couldn't find you upstairs, the security guard told me you were down here."

"I needed a workout." Rand planted his hands on the tile edge and heaved himself out of the water in a glistening display of rippling muscle.

Tara's mouth dried and other parts of her moistened even more than the balmy humidity of the indoor pool area mandated. Her gaze fell to the wet, black swim trunks clinging to and clearly outlining his masculinity. A sliver of untanned skin at his waistband made her yearn to reach out and trace the pale line. With her tongue. Once upon a time she'd been welcome to do exactly that.

She blinked and lifted her gaze back to his face. After only three nights of sleeping with him by her side she'd missed him last night. Missed the sound of his breathing and his warm presence beside her beneath the covers. But it was more than just a means to ending the loneliness that had consumed her since she'd lost her mother. She'd missed Rand.

"Why do you hate cruising?" she repeated.

He reached for the towel in the chair beside hers and dragged it over his skin. "Does it matter?"

"It does to me."

He hesitated and shifted his gaze to the mural of leaping dolphins on the far wall. "When I worked onboard I always had the least desirable accommodations. The ones my father refused to inflict on a crew member. Usually a small interior cabin in the noisiest part of the ship. No porthole. I rarely saw the horizon unless I made a point to walk the decks between shifts."

"That sounds like solitary confinement."

"An apt description."

Pieces of the Rand Kincaid puzzle clicked together and she

didn't like the picture forming. Had she known Everett Kincaid at all? She added another mental tick in the "no" column.

"During our cruise you only returned to the cabin to sleep or change clothes. And you always kept the drapes open."

His hard gaze returned to hers. "Is there a point to your chatter?"

"I thought you were avoiding being alone with me."

"I was."

She winced. "You rearranged the furniture at the office and at home so your desks face the window, and you won't let me close the blinds in your office even when the afternoon sun glares on your computer screen."

Now she knew why and her heart squeezed. The plants she'd added to block the late afternoon rays wouldn't cure this problem.

Rand remained silent. His muscles corded with tension. "We have an early meeting to prepare for."

She ignored his attempt to derail the conversation. "You're claustrophobic. Because of Everett. Because of what he did to you."

"I am not claustrophobic. I ride in elevators every day."

This man who hated weakness had one of his own—one he refused to acknowledge even to himself.

Even though his body language discouraged sympathy, she couldn't help but offer it. If anybody ever needed to be held, Rand did. Regardless of his still damp body, she moved forward and wrapped her arms around him.

He stiffened. "Tara—"

She tilted back her head so she could see his face and he could see hers. He needed to know she didn't think less of him because he wasn't perfect. "I don't know what Everett hoped to gain by treating you that way. But it was wrong."

He dropped the towel in the chair and caught her shoulders. But instead of pushing her away he stared into her eyes for long, silent seconds. His eyes probed hers as if he were trying to see inside her. And then he bent and covered her mouth with his. The kiss wasn't hard or seductive or even hungry like the ones they'd shared before. This one was gentle, tender and so soft that tears pricked behind her eyelids.

He slowly lifted his head, his lips clinging to hers for precious seconds.

A door opened behind her and a pair of KCL employees entered, breaking whatever connection she and Rand had just made. He lowered his hands and stepped away. "I'll be upstairs in ten minutes. Order breakfast. We'll eat together."

Feeling as if the blinders had been ripped from her eyes, Tara headed upstairs. Rand had good reason to hate his father.

Tara was beginning to hate him, too. Because Everett Kincaid had a cruel side she'd never suspected.

"How are you?" Rand said into his cell phone as he leaned back in his office chair late Tuesday afternoon.

"So you do remember how to use a phone. Nice to know. I'm fine. How are you, big brother?"

The sarcasm in Nadia's voice hit its target. She hadn't forgiven him for five years of neglect. "Nadia, I couldn't call."

"I know you couldn't call Mitch because he might mention it to Dad, but you could have called me, Rand."

"I knew Mitch would look out for you."

"I didn't want to talk to Mitch. I wanted to talk to you. You could have at least let me know you were okay."

Despite their six-year age difference Rand and Nadia had been close before he left Miami. She'd never gone to their father with her problems. She'd come to Rand. His refusal to return her calls after he'd abandoned KCL had closed that door. But he'd known breaking that connection was the only way to protect her from their father's scheming machinations to get back at his oldest son.

He massaged the stiff back of his neck. "I'm worried about you. You've been down there a month. Alone."

"I'm fine, and despite a surplus of my own boring company and my shrink's too-frequent calls, I'm not suicidal. *Yet.*"

Alarm blasted through him. He bolted upright. "I'm coming to Dallas."

"I'm kidding. Don't screw up this stupid will clause because of me. I'm fine. Really. I'm not Mom. I'm not going to kill myself."

A chill raced over him. There were some things they had never discussed. Their mother's death was one of them. His gaze shot to the open door between his office and Tara's. He rose, crossed the room and closed it. "What are you talking about?"

Silence greeted him. His mother's and Serita's faces flashed like strobe lights in his mind.

"Nadia, talk to me."

"You didn't know?" she asked in a quiet, tentative tone.

A sick feeling churned in his stomach. "Know what?"

"That mom was…unstable."

"You were only eight when Mom died. You don't know what you're talking about."

"Dad told me. After Lucas…"

The lying son of a bitch. Rand fought to keep his fury out of his voice. "After Lucas and your baby died."

"Yes. I'm sorry, Rand. I thought you knew. Everybody said you were the closest to Mom. After…my accident Dad sent me to a shrink. He was afraid Mom's illness ran in the family and that I wouldn't be able to deal with losing Lucas and our baby. At Dad's insistence I've been seeing a shrink monthly ever since. I guess that's one thing I won't miss now that Dad's gone. I can finally get out of therapy."

Her laugh sounded hollow.

The pain in his jaw made Rand unclench his teeth. "Our mother's only problem was him. The lying, cheating jerk she married."

More silence. "No, Rand, Mom was manic depressive with a touch of paranoia thrown in. I know because after the accident the doctors tested me every which way but Sunday to make sure I wasn't the same. When I realized they were giving me a mental health exam I clammed up and refused to answer any more questions until they leveled with me. Dad allowed them to tell me about Mom."

Rand closed his eyes and pinched the bridge of his nose. Denial steamed through every pore. "That sounds like some of Dad's usual manipulative bull "

"It's not. According to the doctor Mom was fine when she stayed on her meds, but sometimes she'd become convinced Dad was trying to control her by drugging her and she'd go off them."

If that were true, then it explained some of his mother's erratic behavior. Most of the time she'd be a happy and normal mom, other times she'd be a clingy and morose woman who tearfully railed about her husband's sins to her oldest son. Had her conviction that her husband was cheating on her been paranoia or fact? His father had certainly tomcatted around since her death.

"I'm sorry if I tainted your memories of Mom."

"You didn't. I knew—" He swallowed. After years of secrecy, it was time to come clean. "I knew hitting the tree wasn't an accident. I didn't realize anyone else knew."

"I suspect that's because to Dad appearances were everything. Like that stupid portrait hanging in the living room at Kincaid Manor, we always had to look and act like the perfect family. And Rand, from the conversations I've overheard over the years, Dad knew. I think he might have paid someone to make sure the police reports said 'accident,' but I'm not sure. You know how he was. He always refused to discuss anything with me."

"Bribing someone and refusing to admit it sounds like him." Rand shoved a hand through his hair and paced. "I should have stopped her that night, Nadia. I knew Mom was drunk and upset over Dad's latest bimbo. I should have taken the keys to all the cars to bed with me. Not just her keys."

Nadia's gasp carried down the line as clearly as if she'd been in the room beside him. "How can you blame yourself? Rand, you were *fourteen*. And she was determined. If you'd stopped her that night then there would have been another night."

"No. I could have stopped her," he repeated.

"God, I hate doing this," she muttered almost inaudibly. "Do you know how many times she tried to kill herself?"

Rand's heart slammed hard against his ribs. His fingernails dug into his palms. "She tried more than once?"

"Yes. Do you remember the vacations she'd go on alone?"

Everything seemed to slow to a crawl, even the KCL ship he could see departing port via Government Cut moved in slow motion.

Memories flashed through his mind. *Your father thinks I need time away. I think he just wants me out of the house so he can entertain his girlfriend.*

He wiped a hand down his face. "Yes."

"Apparently, those were inpatient treatments."

"You don't know that. You were too young. It started before you were out of diapers."

"I know what my doctors told me."

A fist closed in his gut. He should have known. "I should have done something."

"Rand, listen to yourself. You were the kid. She was the adult. She was supposed to be responsible for you. Not the other way around. And since Mom apparently wasn't capable, we had Mrs. Duncan."

Mrs. Duncan, the housekeeper/guard dog who, as far as he knew, still ruled Kincaid Manor. "If I'd told Dad—"

"God, Rand Kincaid, you are just like him."

Not what he wanted to hear.

"You want to control the world. Well, you can't."

Rand bristled at the words she practically shouted at him, but before he could object, Nadia continued, "Look, I know you probably won't believe this, but Dad loved Mom, and he did everything within his power to keep her from hurting herself. I don't think he cheated on her."

No, Rand didn't believe it. Not after hearing his mother's tearful rants. He'd borne the guilt over his mother's death for so long he couldn't shirk it that easily, and he didn't want to trust this new information. "I repeat, you can't know that. You were only a kid."

"Maybe I don't have the memories of Mom that you have, but I know firsthand that Dad was almost obsessive about making sure we were mentally tougher than she was. I dealt with his smothering watchdog approach after my accident. I know that was ten years after Mom's death, but still, the protective trait was there."

His father had an obsession over their mental health? Was that why he'd tested Rand at every turn? Or had Everett Kincaid pushed his oldest son because the Kincaid patriarch was a twisted tyrant? Rand would never know. The only one with the answers had been cremated and had his ashes scattered in the Gulf Stream.

"I want to talk to Mom's doctors. Give me their names."

"You can't. They're dead. But mine has Mom's medical records and I've read them. That's how I know about every conversation Dad had with her doctor and every hospitalization. They're all documented. I can get a copy for you if you insist."

The story was too far from what he'd believed for years for him to swallow it so easily. "Her doctor shared confidential records?"

"I convinced my shrink that I needed to be informed and educated so I'd know what behaviors to look for if I started slipping."

Fear raced up his spine like an electric current, and the back of his neck prickled. "Is that likely? You slipping?"

"No, Rand, I'm okay. Really, truly okay. We all are. I just needed to understand why sometimes my mother loved me and sometimes she couldn't seem to stand the sight of me."

A crushing sensation settled on his chest. Why hadn't they had this discussion years ago? "I know what you mean."

"And while I'm rocking your world, I guess I should tell you Dad admitted 'Uncle Robert' was really a pediatric shrink, and he came around to make sure we were okay after Mom died and that we hadn't inherited her illness. As you said, I was only eight, so I barely remember him, but you probably do."

Rand recalled the gray-haired man who'd come to dinner often over a period of months and asked a lot of questions. Rand had believed it was because their father's friend was genuinely interested in the Kincaid siblings' comings and goings—more so than their own father, who'd usually remained mute and steely-eyed during the long meals.

"The one Dad said was a friend from college." And now that Rand thought about it, the guy was pretty old to be one of their father's classmates.

"Yes, he's the one. Now can we switch to a less morose subject? Like how is my replacement working out?"

Rand had more questions. And he would ask them. Another

time. After he'd digested this series of bombshells. Nadia's revelations had tilted his whole world on its axis and jeopardized everything he thought he knew.

"Julie's good, Nadia. But we have another problem." His new leather chair creaked as he sat at his desk and pulled the data Tara had gathered forward.

He outlined the investigation and his suspicions. For several moments the discussion focused on areas Nadia suggested he examine more closely. She spoke so fast Rand hoped he could decipher his hastily written notes later.

And then she paused. "I can hear by the way you talk about Tara that you're falling for her again."

His pen stabbed a hole in the legal pad. "You're mistaken."

He didn't do love and the idea of letting Tara love him scared the hell out of him.

"Please don't hurt her again, Rand. She's deserves better than the way you treated her last time."

He bit his tongue on telling Nadia exactly what her friend had done.

"You know I can't risk anything permanent with her. Not with my track record."

"You mean Serita?"

"Yes."

"Call her, Rand. Get Serita's side of the story. I think you'll be surprised at what she has to say about that night."

He balked. "I don't want to reopen old wounds."

"Trust me on this. You need to call her."

This morning Tara had tried to get into his head with her nonsense about claustrophobia, and now Nadia wanted to probe his psyche. Not his idea of fun.

He ended his discussion with Nadia and sat staring at the phone number she'd given him as if it were a coiled snake. His mind grappled with the possibility that his mother's death might not have been his fault and that his father might not have been the most unfaithful ass east of the Mississippi.

If he'd been wrong about those—and he wasn't convinced he was—then what else might he be wrong about?

It had taken Rand twenty-four hours to admit Nadia was right. Until he resolved his past it would govern his future.

He reached for the phone and punched in Serita's number with an unsteady hand. Dread weighted his gut like ballast.

"Serita's zoo."

The familiar cheerful voice hit him like a sucker punch, knocking the words from his tongue.

"Hello? Anyone there?"

He could hear children in the background. He cleared his throat. "Serita, it's Rand Kincaid."

"Oh, my gosh. Rand. How are you? Did you know the reunion committee—of which I'm in charge—has been searching high and low for you?"

"No. I've been in California until recently. Serita, I…need to know how you are."

"How long do you have?" She laughed. "Let's see. I'm married. Billy and I have three little hellions, hence the Serita's zoo greeting, and we live outside Kissimmee." She paused. "But that's not what you're asking. Is it?"

"I need to know about that night."

"It wasn't your fault, Rand. Nadia always said— Oops."

His sister's suggestion to call suddenly made sense. "You've kept in touch with Nadia?"

"She's the class agent for her year. I am for ours. And class representatives talk. Okay, here's the abbreviated version. I faked a suicide attempt because I was ticked off with my parents. All of my friends were going away to college and my overprotective parents wouldn't let me. And being a drama queen, I reacted by doing the one thing guaranteed to make my folks crack down even tighter. Dumb, huh? And of course, I am paying now because my oldest daughter is just like me."

Faked. Stunned, he leaned back in his chair.

"Rand? You did the right thing in breaking up with me. We were too young to get serious, and I was way too immature. Besides, if I'd married you, I never would have met Billy. And he's the one I was meant to be with. He's my Prince Charming."

He heard satisfaction and happiness in Serita's voice, and a load of guilt lifted from his shoulders. "I'm glad you're okay."

"Oh, buggers. Little Billy's splashing in the potty again. Gotta go. Keep in touch. And I expect to see you at the next reunion. No excuses."

The dial tone sounded.

Rand stared at the receiver and slowly cradled it. The one-two punch of his telephone conversations with Serita and Nadia left him reeling but also feeling lighter than he had in decades. He hadn't been the cause of Serita's self-destructive behavior, and according to Nadia, the blame for his mother's death couldn't be laid at his door, either.

That left Tara. If she'd been a victim of his father's machinations, could he blame her? Look how the SOB had made Rand jump through hoops, and Rand was no naive pushover.

Forgiveness no longer seemed too much to ask.

It was time to take a chance on a relationship with Tara. He wasn't thinking marriage or even long-term. His head wasn't ready to take that leap yet, but for the first time in his life, the possibility of a relationship measured in weeks or months instead of hours or days, was there. And Tara had proven through standing by her mother and by not taking any crap from Rand that she was strong enough to handle whatever the future held.

He shut down his computer and locked away the notes on

his exchange with Nadia. Anticipation seeped into his blood-stream. Anticipation of an evening with Tara.

Showing Tara a good time had always resulted in a good time for him. She'd been the one who'd helped him defuse the tension when the battles with his father had become too much. And she'd done it again in the past two weeks. With the Jet Ski ride, the stupid hula lessons and even letting him mow her grass.

He shot to his feet, crossed the room and yanked open his door. "Grab your stuff and let's go."

Tara startled and glanced at her watch. "It's barely five."

"We're leaving. Lock up."

"Let me pack the confidential files to work on tonight."

"No. No work tonight."

Her confusion over his deviation from the norm of working almost around the clock showed in her puckered brow and the teeth pinching her bottom lip. "Did you decide to turn every-thing over to a forensic accountant like we discussed?"

"Not yet."

She shut down her computer, locked away the files and re-trieved her purse.

"Where are we going?" she asked as she rose.

"Home. To bed."

Her eyes went wide and her purse slipped from her fingers and bounced off her shoe. Rand bent, snatched it up and handed it to her. Heat pooled in his groin. He planned to make love to Tara tonight without holding back. It was time. Hell, past time. "Ready?"

"Yes."

Hope flared in her big, blue eyes, and for the first time, Rand didn't feel an urgent need to crush it with caustic words.

Ten

Had she imagined the look in Rand's eyes?

By the time she and Rand had made the twenty-five-minute drive to her house in his Porsche convertible Tara had convinced herself she'd made a mistake. The roar of the wind and the sounds of traffic during the ride had made conversation difficult. She had no barometer to measure his strange mood.

Her legs trembled as she traversed the sidewalk leading to her front door. She lifted a trembling hand to smooth her windblown hair. He caught it, pulled her behind the bougainvillea screening her front porch from the street and backed her against the porch post. His hands cupped her face, holding her while he studied her as if memorizing her features. His thumbs skated over her cheekbones.

Anticipation tempered with desire and something softer, warmer and sweeter than anything she'd ever seen from Rand before simmered in his eyes.

No. She hadn't made a mistake.

Her heart skipped erratically. Hope filled her chest and bathed her with a heat far stronger than the summer sun's evening glow. She dampened her lips and his eyes tracked the movement.

He bent his head and touched his lips to hers in a kiss so gentle, so fleeting, she sighed.

"Let's take this inside."

The gravelly timbre of his voice whipped her hormones into a frenzy. Whatever had come over him, she liked it, and she wasn't about to argue.

Rand unlocked the door, ushered her over the threshold and then reengaged the lock with a quick flick of his wrist. Without a word he laced his fingers through hers and led her upstairs to her bedroom. Her pulse raced, and it had nothing to do with his swift ascent of the stairs.

In her room he shrugged out of his suit coat and tossed it on a chair, and then he took her purse and sent it in the same direction.

"Rand?" She kept waiting for one of his barbs—the ones she'd finally figured out he used to push her away whenever she got too close.

He lifted his hands and removed the pins from her hair, dropping them on the bedside table. When he finished, he finger-combed her curls. "I like it short."

"Thank you?"

"It's sexy. Makes it easy for me to do this." He buried his face in her neck. His five o'clock shadow pricked deliciously beneath her ear, contrasting with the soft touch of his lips, the erotic scrape of his teeth along her tendon and the slick heat of his tongue.

She shivered and hooked her fingers over his belt for balance. He found her zipper and lowered it. Cool air dusted her spine. And then he straightened and pulled her fuchsia sheath dress over her head, leaving her in the matching fuchsia bikini-panty-and-bra set she'd bought specifically with him in mind. The flare of his nostrils and his expanding pupils told her he liked the semi-sheer lace. Her dress landed somewhere near the chair, but his eyes never left her and hers never left his.

His hands clasped her hips and his thumbs caressed the sensitive skin beneath her navel. Goose bumps lifted her skin.

She covered his hands. "Rand, what's going on?"

He looked deep into her eyes. "We're going to do something that's overdue. We're going to make love in your bed. All night long."

Her breath stalled in her chest and the blood drained from her head. She felt wobbly and weak. He'd said *make love* instead of *have sex* or, even worse, *do her.*

Did that mean what she thought it meant? She was afraid to let herself hope. She'd hoped for miracles before, with Rand, with her mother, and she'd been the loser both times.

Tara's bold, new courage deserted her. She couldn't ask for clarification. Because his reply could be the answer to her prayers. Or the end of her dreams. But she could show him what she wanted him to mean.

She reached up, curled her fingers around his neck and brought his lips to hers. He took her mouth in a hot, hungry kiss, raking his hands up and down her bare back, and she poured every ounce of feeling she had into her response.

A flick of his fingers loosened her bra. When he broke the kiss and pulled back slightly to remove it she shoved her hands between them and tackled the buttons of his shirt. Concentrating on the task wasn't easy with his hands shaping her breasts and buffing the sensitive tips. Once she had his shirt open and his shirttails free, she burrowed herself against his skin, absorbing his heat and relishing the tickle of his chest hair on her tightly beaded nipples.

Rand released her long enough to deal with his cuffs and then he removed his shirt. His gaze devoured her, her breasts, her panties, her legs, her face. She'd waited years to see that look of pure, unrestrained passion aimed at her from those hazel eyes.

She loosened his leather belt buckle and his pants and eagerly shoved the fabric down his thighs. His hands mimicked her actions, skimming her panties over her hips. The lace pooled at her ankles. She kicked her sandals and panties out of the way, and stood naked before him in the bright sunlight streaming through the windows. She suddenly felt self-conscious and crossed her arms. Each time they'd made love the room had either been dimly lit or dark.

"Don't. You look beautiful. You were gorgeous before, but now…" He pursed his lips and let out a silent whistle. "Stunning."

She basked in the words, but even more so in the approval and hunger in his eyes. This was what she'd wanted from him five years ago when he'd swept her off her feet and what she wanted even more now. And with every passing second she wanted to believe in miracles.

He sat on the mattress to remove his shoes. Tara quickly knelt in front of him and took over the task. Her fingers trembled, but as soon as the wingtips, socks and pants were history she rose, eager to hold him, to be as close to him as she possibly could be.

Instead of standing, Rand grasped her waist and pulled her between his legs to lave her breast with his tongue. She shifted impatiently as he circled, grazed, sucked and caressed, but he wouldn't be rushed. One big hand splayed across her bottom, alternately kneading her flesh and caressing her crevice. The other combed through her curls, found her slickness and stroked, igniting the desire smoldering low in her belly.

She tangled her fingers in his hair, then shaped his brow, cheekbones, stubbled jaw and strong neck while he worked magic with his hands and mouth. The tremors started deep within her. She didn't want to peak alone this time. She wanted to share that moment with Rand, for she truly would be making love.

She dug her nails into his broad shoulders, wiggled free of his embrace and opened the nightstand drawer. After locating a condom she knelt again to roll it over his hard, smooth flesh. His hands dug into the edge of the mattress. His chest and his penis expanded. His scent—part arousal, part Rand—filled her senses.

And then he bolted to his feet, pulling her with him and into his arms. The heat of his body scalded her and his caressing hands lit trails of fire over her skin. His kisses devoured her with sweeps and swirls of his tongue and left her with a head-spinning shortage of oxygen. She clung to him, stroked him, his shoulders, his back, his buttocks, his upper thighs—every supple, taut inch within reach.

She couldn't get enough of him and the feeling seemed mutual. There was a desperate edge to his hunger that she didn't understand, but her body responded in kind. And when his thigh thrust between hers, she welcomed the pressure, curled her fingers into his waist and her moan poured into his mouth.

He lifted his head, ripped back the covers and swept her into his arms to lay her in the center of the mattress. Tara eagerly opened her arms. He settled in the cradle of her legs and paused for precious heart-pounding moments on the brink of joining them.

His gaze locked with hers and he slowly filled her until she was so full emotion nearly burst from her. She ached to blurt out her feelings, to release the floodgates on the words of love waiting on the tip of her tongue. But the last time she'd done that she'd driven him away. And she couldn't risk that now.

Biting her tongue, she let her touch do the talking, silently whispering the words with each caress, every kiss, each tilt of her hips as she took him deeper into her core and into her soul. Into her heart.

She immersed herself in the heat of his skin, the power of his body and the taste of him. With each passing second she loved him more. And she started to believe in a future with Rand.

Each powerful thrust increased the tension inside her and every withdrawal left her gasping and aching for his return. She wrapped her arms and legs around him, holding him close and trying to get closer still.

And then release showered over her, tightening and releasing her muscles, tingling her toes and her flesh and stealing her breath. Rand stiffened in her arms and threw back his head. His face contorted with pleasure as he joined her.

Several pounding heartbeats later his eyes opened and found hers again. He lowered slowly, reverently, to kiss her brow, her nose, her mouth. Sliding to her side, he pulled her into his arms and held her tightly, in a way he hadn't before. He nuzzled her temple, stroked her back. Every gentle caress made her feel cherished and loved in a way she never had. Her breathing eventually returned to normal and the moisture on her skin evaporated. She braced herself for his departure, but he didn't pull away.

This was exactly how she wanted her relationship with Rand to be. The passion. The spontaneity. The connection. They'd had the first two last time around, and this time she wanted them all. This union had shown her what could be and it was so much more satisfying than the sex they'd had on the cruise.

Rand leaned back, separating their upper bodies only far enough to meet her gaze. She was certain her love shone in her eyes. There was no possible way to contain it and she didn't even try. Happiness bubbled within her and she couldn't stop a broad smile.

He cupped her cheek. "I know why you did it. And I don't blame you."

Confused, Tara blinked. "Did what?"

Revulsion flickered across Rand's face so quickly she almost missed it. But she hadn't. And that glimpse sent a frisson over her. Her smile faded and her muscles tensed.

"Slept with my father."

Her heart stuttered and her heated body chilled. "I told you I never slept with Everett."

"It's okay, Tara. I forgive you."

Tara scrambled out of his arms and out of the bed. "You can't forgive me for something I didn't do."

He sat up. The sheet fell away to reveal every inch of him. "You don't have to be ashamed. We can put it behind us and forget it ever happened. It's okay. I understand."

"No. You don't. You don't have a clue what happened that night."

"You don't have to lie."

Her dream of a future with Rand gave a last gasp and died. She closed her eyes and let her head fall back as she realized her mistake. She hadn't earned his trust now or then. Both times she'd rushed the relationship, counting on the physical bond leading his heart into an emotional commitment. She'd given him everything—her body and her heart—before he was ready to accept them.

He didn't trust her. And he probably never would. Nothing she could say would convince him she hadn't betrayed him.

Feeling exposed, she ducked into the bathroom, snatched her robe off the hook on the back of the door and shoved her arms into the sleeves. Her hands fumbled so badly it took three tries to tie the slippery satiny sash.

Rand stood by the bed when she returned. Naked. Powerful.

"Without trust, Rand, you have nothing. And that's what we have. Nothing." She'd gambled and she'd lost. A sob built in her chest. She fought to contain it, gulping it back, but it only rose again. She forced calming air through her nose and into her lungs, but it hurt. Everything hurt. It hurt to think, to stand here and look at the beautiful bronzed body of the man she'd wanted to share her life, her home and her heart with.

And it nearly crushed her to admit defeat. But this was a battle she couldn't win.

"Get out. Out of my room. Out of my house."

Rand stiffened and a muscle in his jaw ticked. "What about KCL and the terms of my father's will?"

The question carved another chunk out of her heart. His first concern wasn't about her or them, but about the business.

"That you'd even have to ask only proves my point. You don't know me at all. I'm going to take a shower. When I get out, I want you to be gone."

A gurgle of noise jolted Rand awake.

Bleary-eyed, he tracked the sound to the coffeepot. Set on timer. By Tara.

Tara.

Why in the hell couldn't she admit she'd made a mistake and been led astray by his father? Rand could live with mistakes, but not with lies. Dishonesty was a deal breaker.

Focusing on his anger and trying to ignore the strange ache in his chest and the hammers pounding in his head, he swung his legs off the leather sofa, planted his feet on the rug Tara had chosen and scrubbed his hands up his face and through his hair.

If what Nadia had said was true, he wasn't to blame for their mother's death. But he'd sure as hell cost them their inheritance by trying to force a confession out of Tara.

Could he live with that failure?

No.

But his sleep-deprived brain refused to cough up an accept-able alternative. Once he had a pot of coffee onboard to coun-teract the two hours of sleep he'd had, he was going to come up with a strategy to fix the situation.

If he could.

Not *if*, dammit. He would.

The only way to hold on to KCL, Kincaid Manor and his father's hefty investment portfolio was to convince Tara to stay on as his PA. Not an easy feat since he'd called her a liar in bed.

Could he work with a liar?

For Nadia's and Mitch's sakes he'd find a way. But per-sonally, he and Tara were finished. Unless she came clean.

She cared about him. He'd seen it in her eyes, felt it in her touch, tasted it on her lips. They made a good team. In the office and out of it. Why ruin a successful relationship when he was offering forgiveness? What did she have to gain by lying?

The questions nagged him because Tara's actions weren't logical. But he didn't have the answers.

He stood and tried to stretch the kinks from his spine. Outside the wall of windows the sun rose over the bay and the Atlantic beyond Government Cut, the channel used by KCL ships. He could have gone to a hotel or to Kincaid Manor last night, but he'd needed time alone to think and something to occupy his mind. What better than the Rendezvous puzzle?

He'd stayed up most of the night, poring over the docu-ments Tara had compiled and reading the notes she'd jotted in the margins. After comparing her findings with Nadia's suggestions he'd spotted a clear trail that should eventually lead to who'd been embezzling from KCL.

He wanted to run his theory by Tara. Without her to share his hypothesis the discovery lacked the punch he usually felt before closing a deal. She'd become an important part of his team.

But Tara wasn't here.

Needing a cold shower to clear his head and wash the grit from his eyes, he made his way to the en suite bathroom. Once again, Tara's touch reminded him of what he'd lost because of her stubborn refusal to confess. She'd stocked his private bath with everything he could possibly need, from toothpaste to razors to clean towels and even an unopened bottle of his cologne. He wouldn't even need to fetch his shaving kit from his car.

Extracting the clean suit, shirt and tie she'd insisted he keep in the closet Rand stripped, showered, shaved and dressed. He paused in front of the mirror, tightened the knot of his tie and squared his shoulders.

He'd made Tara an offer she couldn't refuse once before. He'd do it again. And if her demands were unreasonable he'd sic the legal department on her. She'd signed an employment contract and he'd hold her to it.

He stepped out of the bathroom, picked up the mug that Tara had selected. A sound in the outer office stilled his hand before he could pour the brew. He glanced at his watch. Eight. No one should be here this early. And since Tara had kept the confidential documents locked in her desk, whoever was out there was breaching security.

Luckily, he'd had a duplicate key to her desk and the documents were in his office now. He stealthily crossed to the open door and jerked to a halt.

Tara. She bent over her desk, depositing her purse in the drawer.

A rush of something warm and soothing and energizing and...*good* that he couldn't identify suffused him. He tamped down the unacceptable flood of emotions. She'd probably come to clean out her desk. The signed letter of recommendation he'd written would make leaving easier——until he involved the legal team.

An ugly thought snuck up on him. Had she asked for that letter because she planned to leave him in the lurch all along to get even for him dumping her years ago?

Vindictiveness didn't seem to be Tara's style.

"I didn't expect to see you today."

She startled and turned a pale face in his direction. Despite heavier than usual makeup, bruised circles shadowed the area beneath her eyes. "I gave you my word I'd see this year through. But we're boss/employee from now on and that's it."

His thoughts exactly. So why did he experience a sudden and irritating jab of dissatisfaction? "You're not quitting?"

"Not unless you fire me."

He'd take the reprieve any way he could get it. It meant one less battle he had to win. "I need you to finish the year."

The urge to sink his fingers into the soft golden curls she hadn't bothered to scrape back this morning and kiss her in gratitude wasn't welcome. He'd sworn off getting personal with her this time around. Her lips were off-limits.

"Your car was in the parking garage. How did you get here?"

"I took a taxi." She sat in her chair and booted up her computer as if last night hadn't happened. But her cool tone, her steel-beam-straight spine and her tense features implied anger. What did she have to be angry about? He was the one who'd been wronged.

Did she feel ashamed and guilty for turning to his father? He understood guilt. He'd lived with it for two decades. But he'd offered to wipe the slate clean. All she had to do was admit——

His thoughts stopped dead in the water like a ship running aground. He backtracked over last night's words. She'd said that if he had to ask her intentions toward KCL, he didn't know her.

She'd promised him a year. And here she was.

Would a woman who kept her promises lie?

Once again, the facts didn't add up. But if Tara hadn't lied... No, she had. He'd seen the proof. "Tara—"

"The Rendezvous file isn't in my drawer," she interrupted. "Do you have it?"

"Yes. But—"

"I wasn't finished with my calculations. May I have it back?"

"Not yet." Determined to make sense of her illogical behavior, he planted a hand on each side of her U-shaped workstation, blocking her in. "Tara—"

"What in the hell is going on?" Mitch demanded from the doorway. "Security says you slept in your office last night."

Frustrated by the interruption, Rand peeled his gaze from the surprise in Tara's eyes to his brother. "What of it?"

"Did you?"

He straightened. "Yes."

Mitch looked ready to explode. But anger couldn't cover the worry in his brother's eyes as he looked from Rand to Tara and back. "Could I speak to you privately?"

Rand stared at Tara, who swiveled her chair, turned her back on him and picked up the phone. She was back onboard as his PA, and he wasn't going to screw that up. She wanted business only? Fine. He couldn't agree more.

Liar.

He'd miss her, he admitted reluctantly. He'd miss trying to follow the sharp and sometimes convoluted way her mind worked. He'd miss playing with her. Having sex with her.

He'd never before had an intimate encounter as satisfying as he'd had last night. Ever. His blood heated and headed south of his belt. All he had to do was recall the end of the evening to derail his hormones.

"Hold my calls." He led Mitch into the office and shut the door. "I talked to Nadia yesterday."

"What's going on?"

"She claims she's fine."

"That's not what I meant and you know it. With you and Tara."

His molars clamped together. "None of your business."

"It's my business if you're going to screw up. I warned you not to let your personal relationship cause problems. Did you?"

"She's here, isn't she?"

"You slept in your office and your car is loaded with suitcases. Either she threw you out or you moved out."

Not something he'd confirm or deny.

"Do you want to move in to the manor?"

"You have a full house. I'll find a place. Can we talk KCL business? Or is this a social club?" Even before Mitch's shoulders snapped back and his chin thrust forward, Rand regretted his harsh words. He rubbed his throbbing temple, then filled his coffee mug and a second one for Mitch, hoping caffeine would nix his headache.

He pointed at the papers he'd left spread across the coffee table/ottoman when he'd finally given up and closed his eyes last night. Correction. This morning. "Have a seat and take a look. Nadia gave me a list of places to check records. I put those calculations together with Tara's, and we have a warm trail to turn over to a forensic accountant."

He strode to the windows and stared out at the water while he sipped his coffee. Behind him he heard the shuffle of papers and the clicking of calculator keys as Mitch went over the entries. If only the situation with Tara was as easy to comprehend as the columns of fabricated numbers. But no such luck. Rand had his work cut out for him. Keeping Tara happy. Keeping her here. Defining new boundaries. Controlling his hormones.

Good thing he enjoyed a challenge.

"These are Tara's notes?" Mitch asked ten minutes later.

Rand turned. "Yes."

"She's good. Too smart to be a PA."

Pride filled Rand. Pride he didn't have a right to feel. He couldn't take any credit for Tara's intelligence. "I noticed."

"Too smart to fall for Dad's crap."

"Maybe." He scrubbed his free hand across his nape. Yet another clue that didn't fit. As he'd read through Tara's notes last night he kept asking himself one question. How had his father lured her into the trap? Whatever the bait, it had to have been good. Good enough to lie for. What could Tara be hiding?

"Any chance you misinterpreted what you saw that night?"

A question he'd asked himself a hundred times. "Seeing is believing."

"Unless it's an illusion."

An option he hadn't considered. The hairs on the back of his neck prickled. "You think Dad set me up?"

"It's a possibility, given your history. There was nothing he liked better than testing your limits. Problem is, until the day you walked, you never broke. He'd see that as a challenge."

A test or a betrayal? The only ones who knew the truth were a dead man and the woman in the outer office.

Eleven

She'd rather be alone than with a man who didn't trust her, Tara told herself as she shut down her computer Friday evening.

But being right didn't mean she didn't hurt.

If not for the teamwork she and Rand had shared before their argument, she'd never give a second thought to the change in atmosphere of recent weeks. To anyone else Rand probably seemed like the perfect boss. Cool, detached and impersonal. He'd spoken to her only when necessary. But she'd felt him watching her on too many occasions to count. Watching and waiting. For what, she didn't know.

Not having humiliated herself by blurting out her feelings for Rand when they'd made love that night three *l-o-n-g* weeks ago was cold comfort when she crawled into bed alone each night.

Work. Home. Paying bills. She was right back where she'd started from before Rand Kincaid reentered her life. The only difference was that now she had a job that challenged her and money to pay off her debts to go with her freshly broken heart.

She picked up her pen and made an X over the date. Keeping a promise had never been more difficult, and each day she marked off on the calendar was a bittersweet one. Another day with the man she loved meant one day less until she'd leave him.

The light went out on her phone as Rand ended his call.

"Tara, get in here."

She caught her breath at the sound of his voice and her pulse did that stupid little tripping thing. Again. Would she ever stop loving him?

She rose, smoothed her hands down her hips, picked up her notepad and blanked her expression.

Mitch stood as she entered Rand's office. "Quite the sleuth, aren't you?"

She kept her gaze on him rather than look at Rand because each time she looked into those hazel eyes her heart splintered a new crack. "I'm sorry?"

"The money trail. You enjoyed tracking it."

She shrugged. "If you let me sniff around long enough, I usually find what I'm looking for. It comes from reading all those mysteries to my mother."

Mitch walked toward the door, but paused with his hand on the frame. "It's a shame everyone isn't that bright."

The door closed behind him, leaving her no choice but to face Rand, who stood behind his desk. In general, she avoided looking directly at him by never looking higher than the knot of his tie. Not easy considering they worked nine to ten hours together most days. But she didn't want him reading her heartbreak on her face.

She braced herself and lifted her gaze. He needed a haircut. The dark chocolate-colored strands hung over his white collar.

And he could use a shave, too. Five o'clock shadow darkened his jaw and upper lip. The combination of shaggy hair and stubbled jaw made him look too sexy for words. He'd discarded his suit coat, loosened his tie and rolled up his shirtsleeves.

Silence stretched between them until she thought her nerves would snap. She fought the urge to fidget under his steady stare. "What did he mean by *everyone isn't that bright?*"

"That you've put together all the clues. Using your data the forensic accountant found the embezzlement trail leading not only to Patricia Pottsmith, but also implicating Donald Green, her boss and the president of Rendezvous. The arrest warrants are being served downstairs under Mitch's supervision as we speak."

The news only mildly surprised her. Patricia had always looked out for number one.

Rand came around his desk, crossed to the sofa and indicated she join him.

Tara sat at the far end and fiddled with the pen tucked in the spiral wire of her notebook. If she sat any closer, she'd have to smell him. Too late. The air-conditioning kicked on, carrying a whiff of his cologne to tease her senses. Need rose within her. Need she had every intention of ignoring for the next ten and a half months.

Maybe by the end of the year he'd trust her....

Stop it. You are not going to get your hopes up and dashed again.

"What tipped you off?" Rand asked, making her look at him. She saw triumph in his eyes, but also a glint of something she couldn't identify.

"Patricia said something at the cocktail party about sleeping with her boss. Originally, I thought she meant Everett, but then I tapped in to the KCL gossip grapevine and found out she and Donald often travel together unrelated to KCL business."

"Good job."

His praise hit her like a sunbeam, showering her with warmth. "It's what you paid me to do."

"No, Tara. You went beyond the call of duty on this one. And when we've finished with our year as boss and PA, Mitch and I want you to stay on at KCL."

She bit her lip and hesitated. "Are you staying?"

"Yes."

She wouldn't be able to bear seeing him in the halls or cafeteria. "I don't think—"

"We're creating an assistant director of shared services position for you. You'd get to work with Nadia and track expenditures within each of the brands."

A job and opportunity she'd jump at under any other circumstances.

"It's a promotion," he added when she remained silent.

"Thank you for your confidence in my abilities, but I'll have to pass."

Disappointment flickered across his face.

She wrapped both hands around her notepad and prepared to stand. "Is that all?"

"No." He shifted closer on the sofa, took the notebook from her and tossed it on the ottoman/coffee table. His hands enfolded hers, making her breath hitch and her heart stutter. "I want you to tell me what happened that night."

"Which night?" She knew exactly which one he meant. Her stomach churned.

"The night you *didn't* sleep with my father."

Her lungs refused to function. She finally managed to wheeze in a breath despite the sarcophaguslike constriction of her rib cage. "You believe me?"

"Yes. And I'm the one Mitch is claiming isn't too bright. All the clues have been right in front of me. And I couldn't put them together. You were with my father. But you didn't sleep with him. I get that now. There's not a greedy or selfish bone in your body. The Tara Anthony I know does the right thing, not the easy thing. Like taking a dead-end job so she can make her mother's last months easier and keeping a house because her mother asked her to even though a developer would pay you far in excess of its value to sell.

"Why were you there, Tara? What did my father hold over you to force you into a position where he could take advantage of you?"

If she told him he'd probably despise her for letting her mother die. But she'd already lost him. What did it matter?

"I didn't sleep with Everett that night, Rand. But I wish I had."

"What?" He sat back, his hands fisting by his sides. She could see him fighting to stay calm. But his shock or disgust or whatever you called it was only to be expected.

"Your father offered me a way to possibly save my mother's life. He said he'd take care of her and get her the best oncologist care money could buy if I'd move into Kincaid Manor and become his partner in every way."

He shot to his feet, fury radiating from every clenched muscle in his body. "He used your dying mother to bribe you to become his *mistress?* Damnation, he's sunk to a new low."

She shook her head. But the doubts nagged like a splinter under her skin. "He was lonely. He needed a hostess. And he wanted to help me."

"Tara, he was trying to screw *me* by screwing *you.*"

She flinched. Crudely put. But was it true? She didn't know what to believe anymore. She'd heard so much conflicting information about Everett. And much of it pointed to Everett not being the nice guy she'd believed. How could she have read him so wrong? Look at the deplorable way he'd treated his own son.

She decided she might as well tell Rand the whole pitiful tale so he'd understand why she couldn't accept the plum job he'd offered. "I accepted his proposition, but in the end I couldn't follow through. Because I loved you. I had some crazy, romantic notion that one day you'd come back for me. Dumb. Huh?"

Humiliation burned her cheeks.

She'd waited for Rand like her mother had waited for her father. Tara wondered if that made her loyal or just stupid.

Rand dragged in a slow breath. "You loved me. You weren't lying that night I left you. The first time."

"No. But I lied and said I didn't to try to win you back because I knew you'd refuse my terms if you knew I'd never gotten over you. It was never just about sex for me, Rand. I wanted a chance to make us work. My mother's last words were 'Live your life without regrets.' And I had two. Not fighting for us. And not doing everything I possibly could to help her."

She looked at her hands. "If I'd slept with Everett, I could have bought my mother more time or possibly even saved her life. But I was selfish and I was a coward. It was just sex and I should have been able to do it. That kind of cowardice isn't something you could possibly understand since you were willing to do anything for the ones you loved. Even sleep with me."

He sighed, and it was such a deep, heartfelt sound she had to look at him. "You mean I prostituted myself and you didn't."

"No! You were strong where I was weak. I respect your strength and your sacrifice."

He sat beside her again, closer this time so that his thigh and shoulder brushed hers. "You weren't the coward, Tara. I was. I let you go twice because I was afraid of what could happen if I loved you and let you down.

"My mother committed suicide. I always believed it was because my father was a faithless SOB. And I blamed myself for not finding a way to stop her. I've always been told I was just like my father, a chip off the old block. And when my high school girlfriend ate a bottle of pills after I broke up with her, it reinforced that point. I was a selfish bastard. But I've since learned that my mother's death probably wasn't my father's fault, and it wasn't mine. Serita's faked suicide attempt wasn't, either. But I didn't know that then."

Horrified, she shook her head. "Rand. I would never—"

He covered her mouth with his palm. The warmth of his skin stilled her lips. His other hand cupped her shoulder, holding her in place.

"Let me finish before we're interrupted. I only have about ten minutes before Mitch gets back, and I don't want to share this—*you*—with him.

"I thought I was doing the right thing five years ago by walking away from what we had. I thought I was protecting you. What I didn't factor into the equation was you. You're strong and smart. Too smart to hurt yourself. And you have too much integrity to sleep your way onto Easy Street."

He transferred the hand covering her mouth to her shoulder. "I came back from Europe early to ask my father why he cheated on my mother. I needed to know why he couldn't be faithful. Because after three weeks of trying to forget you, I couldn't. I didn't want to repeat his mistakes by hurting you. I was in love with you, Tara, but I was afraid of what Mitch and I have always called the Kincaid Curse. We Kincaids have a hard time keeping the ones we love."

Surprise rendered her speechless. He'd loved her?

"I've fallen in love with you again. And don't want to lose you."

The emotion and the sincerity in his unwavering gaze made her eyes sting and her throat burn. "You have?"

"Yes. Back then I loved your naivete, your generous spirit, your trusting nature. I loved that you made me forget the stress of the job and showed me how to have fun. Now I love all those things and more. I love your inner strength, your ability to sniff out a crime and your loyalty to my father, Nadia, Mitch and even me despite the fact that I've been a blind idiot and an ass a good part of the time.

"It was because I loved you then that seeing you with my father was such a kick in the teeth. All I could see was that after saying you loved me, you'd turned to the one man I refused to share with. I wasn't rational that night. I was hurt. And I reacted by striking back instead of listening.

"But striking back cost me my family. It cost me KCL. It cost me you. These weeks without you have been hell."

"I've been here every day."

He shook his head. "Not the same. You're physically here and you're giving one hundred percent to your job. But you're not mine. I miss us. I miss you. The apartment I'm living in isn't the only thing that's empty. I am. And I would do anything—*anything*—to get another chance at winning your heart."

Tears welled in her eyes. She blinked them back. But she couldn't crush the hope welling in her chest. "You don't hate me for failing my mother?"

His fingers tightened on her shoulders. "Tara, your mother waited a lifetime for the man she loved to return. What would she have said if you'd told her about my father's offer?"

She swallowed and looked away. "She would have been horrified."

"You had a slim chance of prolonging her life. But would she have wanted to live with the burden of knowing what price you'd paid?"

Her tears spilled over, burning trails down her cheeks, and her chin quivered as she compressed her lips to hold back a sob. She shook her head. "No. She would have hated that."

He swept her tears away with his thumbs and tilted her face until she looked him in the eye. "You didn't let her down, Tara, and you weren't a coward. You held out for what you and she believed in and you continued her legacy of being true to your heart. It would serve me right if I've killed your love and you dumped me. I wouldn't blame you if you walked out. On me and your job. I can survive without KCL. I did it for five years. But I don't want to go another day without waking up beside you."

He dropped to his knee in front of the sofa. "Marry me, Tara. Let me be that man for you, the one you love for eternity. Tell me how to make that happen and I'll do it. Whatever it takes."

Joy bubbled over in a laugh. She cradled his face in her palms and leaned forward to brush a gentle kiss over his lips. "You just did. Yes, Rand, I'll marry you."

She hurled herself into his arms. Rand rose, carrying her with him and lifting her off her feet until they stood hip to hip and heart to heart. He kissed her softly, reverently, and then lifted his head.

Tara smiled up at him. "I am just like my mother. I love you, Rand Kincaid. I always have. And I don't ever intend to stop."

"And I'll be right here beside you, loving you back."

Epilogue

Ten months later

Rand accepted Everett Kincaid's letter from the attorney. He wasn't looking forward to hearing from the dead.

"If you have any questions, please call," Richards said, then left the office.

Rand joined Tara on the leather sofa in his office. She reached for his hand and gave him an encouraging squeeze before passing him the letter opener.

"Do you want to be alone to read this?" Tara asked.

"No. You're part of this. I want you here."

Tara snuggled closer, wrapping her arms around his waist and resting her cheek on his shoulder as he sliced open the envelope. If she noticed his hands were less than steady as he unfolded the sheets written in his father's handwriting she didn't mention it.

He angled the letter so she could read along with him.

Dear Son,

If you're reading this, then you've fulfilled the terms of my will, and you're still at KCL with Tara by your side. And I've gone to wherever it is manipulative old men go when time runs out.

The competition between us drove us apart, but it also made you stronger. I tested you at every turn. I had my reasons. Good ones. You'll have to take my word on that. And you passed every test.

Tara passed her test, too. Five years ago she was in a tight spot and needed money. I offered to be her protector if she'd betray her feelings for you. She refused. Can't say the same for the other women I thought might eventually become my daughter-in-law. I tested them. They failed.

I'm sorry that you had to witness that night and Tara's test. I realize it made you hate me more than you already did. Worse, it drove you and Tara apart. That was never my intention.

For what it's worth, I never cheated on your mother. Wasn't even tempted. I worshipped the ground Mary Elizabeth walked on. But until you feel that kind of love you won't know what I mean. If my plan worked the way I intended, you've found it with Tara by now. She's the right one, son, and the only one worthy of you.

I've watched you since you left my shadow, Rand. You are a man who can stand on his own merits, one who didn't climb the ladder of success due to nepotism. You've earned the right to be CEO of Kincaid Cruise Lines the hard way, and I have no doubt you'll be a better one than I ever was.

I've never said it to your face, and now it's too late, but I'll tell you anyhow.

I love you, son. You've made me proud.

Your father,

Everett Kincaid

He'd waited his entire life to hear those words.

A wad of emotion rose in Rand's throat and nearly choked him. Tara's arms tightened around him. He tilted his head to rest his cheek on her crown and closed his eyes while he struggled to gather his composure.

The letter answered so many questions.

He didn't have to explain about his mother's illness. Tara knew the whole story because it was something she'd needed to know before taking a chance on him. The doctor swore the chances of their children inheriting his mother's illness were slim and Tara had been willing to risk the gamble.

But Tara didn't know about the past women his father had lured away.

He straightened and found empathy and understanding in her damp blue eyes. "He used to steal my girlfriends and then tell me about it in graphic detail. I thought he was just a greedy, sadistic, dirty old man."

"I think you saw what Everett wanted you to see."

"Maybe. But he was wrong. I never wanted to marry any of those other women. Never even considered it. Until you. You're the only one who made me willing to risk the Kincaid Curse."

She smiled. "It makes me feel better to know Everett wasn't really interested in getting me into bed. I can even respect him for looking out for your interests. But I especially like that he plotted to get us back together."

"I owe him for that." Rand kissed her brow. Sharing Tara's home and waking beside her every morning for the past ten months had been a jolt. A pleasant one. And it was a luxury he would never take for granted. "Now that our year's up why don't we take a belated honeymoon? Maybe an extended Hawaiian cruise? Or Polynesia?"

"You hate cruising."

"What better way to get over cabin claustrophobia than by

having a very good reason to stay locked away? You and a bed." He flashed her a naughty grin.

Her face softened. She covered his hand. The sunlight streaming through the office windows flashed on the wedding and engagement rings he'd slipped on her finger six months ago during a private ceremony in the garden she and her mother had nurtured together.

She curled her fingers over his and carried his hand to her stomach. He caressed her, letting her warmth seep through his skin and into his veins. Desire flared within him. Hot. Intense. Predictable. But always new and exciting. The woman got to him without even trying, and it wouldn't be the first time the leather sofa had been used for something besides sitting.

"Maybe we'd better wait on that cruise for a year or two. I'm already a little queasy."

Confused, he frowned. And then the happiness glowing in her eyes hit him like a runaway barge. "You're pregnant?"

Tara beamed, blushed and nodded. "Apparently that night we, um…worked late…" She patted the leather cushion.

The night they'd been too impatient to look for a condom.

Contentment like nothing he'd ever experienced expanded inside him. Rand yanked Tara into his arms and kissed her, but he was grinning so hard it wasn't much of a kiss.

Thanks to his father, he and Tara had a second chance. And Rand wasn't going to let the old man down.

A chuckle rumbled up from his chest. "I wonder what Dad would think about his grandchild being conceived in his office?"

Tara wrinkled her nose. "Knowing Everett, I'm sure he'd find a way to take credit for it."

* * * * *

Don't miss the next story in Emilie Rose's
THE PAYBACK AFFAIRS *series!*
Look for Mitch's book
BOUND BY THE KINCAID BABY
coming in
July 2008 from Silhouette Desire.

THOROUGHBRED LEGACY
*The stakes are high when it comes to love,
horse racing, family secrets
and broken promises.*

*A new exciting Harlequin continuity series
coming soon!*
Led by New York Times *bestselling author*
Elizabeth Bevarly
FLIRTING WITH TROUBLE

Here's a preview!

THE DOOR CLOSED behind them, throwing them into darkness and leaving them utterly alone. And the next thing Daniel knew, he heard himself saying, "Marnie, I'm sorry about the way things turned out in Del Mar."

She said nothing at first, only strode across the room and stared out the window beside him. Although he couldn't see her well in the darkness—he still hadn't switched on a light...but then, neither had she—he imagined her expression was a little preoccupied, a little anxious, a little confused.

Finally, very softly, she said, "Are you?"

He nodded, then, worried she wouldn't be able to see the gesture, added, "Yeah. I am. I should have said goodbye to you."

"Yes, you should have."

Actually, he thought, there were a lot of things he should have done in Del Mar. He'd had *a lot* riding on the Pacific

Classic, and even more on his entry, Little Joe, but after meeting Marnie, the Pacific Classic had been the last thing on Daniel's mind. His loss at Del Mar had pretty much ended his career before it had even begun, and he'd had to start all over again, rebuilding from nothing.

He simply had not then and did not now have room in his life for a woman as potent as Marnie Roberts. He was a horseman first and foremost. From the time he was a schoolboy, he'd known what he wanted to do with his life—be the best possible trainer he could be.

He had to make sure Marnie understood—and he understood, too—why things had ended the way they had eight years ago. He just wished he could find the words to do that. Hell, he wished he could find the *thoughts* to do that.

"You made me forget things, Marnie, things that I really needed to remember. And that scared the hell out of me. Little Joe should have won the Classic. He was by far the best horse entered in that race. But I didn't give him the attention he needed and deserved that week, because all I could think about was you. Hell, when I woke up that morning all I wanted to do was lie there and look at you, and then wake you up and make love to you again. If I hadn't left when I did— the way I did—I might still be lying there in that bed with you, thinking about nothing else."

"And would that be so terrible?" she asked.

"Of course not," he told her. "But that wasn't why I was in Del Mar," he repeated. "I was in Del Mar to win a race. That was my job. And my work was the most important thing to me."

She said nothing for a moment, only studied his face in the darkness as if looking for the answer to a very important question. Finally she asked, "And what's the most important thing to you now, Daniel?"

Wasn't the answer to that obvious? "My work," he answered automatically.

She nodded slowly. "Of course," she said softly. "That is, after all, what you do best."

Her comment, too, puzzled him. She made it sound as if being good at what he did was a bad thing.

She bit her lip thoughtfully, her eyes fixed on his, glimmering in the scant moonlight that was filtering through the window. And damned if Daniel didn't find himself wanting to pull her into his arms and kiss her. But as much as it might have felt as if no time had passed since Del Mar, there were eight years between now and then. And eight years was a long time in the best of circumstances. For Daniel and Marnie, it was virtually a lifetime.

So Daniel turned and started for the door, then halted. He couldn't just walk away and leave things as they were, unsettled. He'd done that eight years ago and regretted it.

"It *was* good to see you again, Marnie," he said softly. And since he was being honest, he added, "I hope we see each other again."

She didn't say anything in response, only stood silhouetted against the window with her arms wrapped around her in a way that made him wonder whether she was doing it because she was cold, or if she just needed something—someone—to hold on to. In either case, Daniel understood. There was an emptiness clinging to him that he suspected would be there for a long time.

* * * * *

THOROUGHBRED LEGACY
coming soon wherever books are sold!

Thoroughbred Legacy

Launching in June 2008

A dramatic new 12-book continuity that embodies the American Dream.

Meet the Prestons, owners of Quest Stables, a successful
horse-racing and breeding empire. But the lives, loves
and reputations of this hardworking family are put at risk
when a breeding scandal unfolds.

Flirting with Trouble

by *New York Times* bestselling author

ELIZABETH BEVARLY

Eight years ago, publicist Marnie Roberts spent seven days
of bliss with Australian horse trainer Daniel Whittleson.
But just as quickly, he disappeared. Now Marnie is
heading to Australia to finally confront the man
she's never been able to forget.

*The stakes are high when it comes to love, horse racing,
family secrets and broken promises.*

A new exciting Harlequin continuity series coming soon!

Cole's Red-Hot Pursuit

Cole Westmoreland is a man who gets what he
wants. And he wants independent and sultry
Patrina Forman! She resists him—until a Montana
blizzard traps them together. For three delicious
nights, Cole indulges Patrina with his brand of
seduction. When the sun comes out, Cole and
Patrina are left to wonder—will this be the end of
the passion that storms between them?

Look for

COLE'S RED-HOT
PURSUIT

by USA TODAY bestselling author

BRENDA
JACKSON

Available in June 2008 wherever you buy books.

Always Powerful, Passionate and Provocative.

REQUEST YOUR FREE BOOKS!

2 FREE NOVELS PLUS 2 FREE GIFTS!

Silhouette® Desire®

Passionate, Powerful, Provocative!

YES! Please send me 2 FREE Silhouette Desire® novels and my 2 FREE gifts (gifts are worth about $10). After receiving them, if I don't wish to receive any more books, I can return the shipping statement marked "cancel". If I don't cancel, I will receive 6 brand-new novels every month and be billed just $4.05 per book in the U.S. or $4.74 per book in Canada, plus 25¢ shipping and handling per book and applicable taxes, if any*. That's a savings of almost 15% off the cover price! I understand that accepting the 2 free books and gifts places me under no obligation to buy anything. I can always return a shipment and cancel at any time. Even if I never buy another book, the two free books and gifts are mine to keep forever.   225 SDN ERVX 326 SDN ERVM

Name _____ (PLEASE PRINT) _____

Address _____ Apt. # _____

City _____ State/Prov. _____ Zip/Postal Code _____

Signature (if under 18, a parent or guardian must sign) _____

Mail to the **Silhouette Reader Service:**
IN U.S.A.: P.O. Box 1867, Buffalo, NY 14240-1867
IN CANADA: P.O. Box 609, Fort Erie, Ontario L2A 5X3

Not valid to current subscribers of Silhouette Desire books.

Want to try two free books from another line?
Call 1-800-873-8635 or visit www.morefreebooks.com.

* Terms and prices subject to change without notice. N.Y. residents add applicable sales tax. Canadian residents will be charged applicable provincial taxes and GST. Offer not valid in Quebec. This offer is limited to one order per household. All orders subject to approval. Credit or debit balances in a customer's account(s) may be offset by any other outstanding balance owed by or to the customer. Please allow 4 to 6 weeks for delivery. Offer available while quantities last.

Your Privacy: Silhouette Books is committed to protecting your privacy. Our Privacy Policy is available online at www.eHarlequin.com or upon request from the Reader Service. From time to time we make our lists of customers available to reputable third parties who may have a product or service of interest to you. If you would prefer we not share your name and address, please check here. ☐

SDES08R

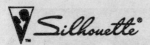

Royal Seductions

Michelle Celmer delivers a powerful miniseries in
Royal Seductions; where two brothers fight for the
crown and discover love. In *The King's Convenient Bride*,
the king discovers his marriage of convenience to the
woman he's been promised to wed is turning all too
real. The playboy prince proposes a mock engagement
to defuse rumors circulating about him and restore
order to the kingdom…until his pretend fiancée
becomes pregnant in *The Illegitimate Prince's Baby*.

Look for

THE KING'S CONVENIENT BRIDE
&
THE ILLEGITIMATE PRINCE'S BABY

BY MICHELLE CELMER

Available in June 2008 wherever you buy books.

Always Powerful, Passionate and Provocative.

COMING NEXT MONTH

#1873 JEALOUSY & A JEWELLED PROPOSITION—
Yvonne Lindsay
Diamonds Down Under
Determined to avenge his family's name, this billionaire sets out
to take over his biggest competition...and realizes his ex may be
the perfect weapon for revenge.

#1874 COLE'S RED-HOT PURSUIT—Brenda Jackson
After a night of passion, a wealthy sheriff will stop at nothing to
get the woman back into his bed. And he always gets what he wants.

#1875 SEDUCED BY THE ENEMY—Sara Orwig
Platinum Grooms
He has a score to settle with his biggest business rival. Seducing
his enemy's daughter proves to be the perfect way to have his
revenge.

#1876 THE KING'S CONVENIENT BRIDE—
Michelle Celmer
Royal Seductions
An arranged marriage turns all too real when the king falls for his
convenient wife. Don't miss the second book in the series, also
available this June!

#1877 THE ILLEGITIMATE PRINCE'S BABY—
Michelle Celmer
Royal Seductions
The playboy prince proposes a mock engagement...until his
pretend fiancée becomes pregnant! Don't miss the first book in
this series, also on sale this June!

#1878 RICH MAN'S FAKE FIANCÉE—Catherine Mann
The Landis Brothers
Caught in a web of tabloid lies, their only recourse is a fake
engagement. But the passion they feel for one another is all
too real.

SDCNM0508